What t.  ...are saying...

5 Angels! "*Me Tarzan, You Jewel* is a sequel to Jennie in the Bottle and is a fabulous continuation... I absolutely loved this story! Thanks to Ms. Ladley for a great read!" ~ *Serena for Fallen Angel Reviews*

"Readers make sure you read this book with a tall glass of ice water nearby. Ms. Ladley writes of carnal lust and a love that cannot be denied... Get ready for an unforgettable trip to Carnal Island." ~ *Darnée for Coffee Time Romance*

"Titania Ladley writes a truly enjoyable story." ~ *Tammy Adams for EarthChildSeries/Novelspot Romance Reviews*

"Let your imagination run free in this entertaining and creative story... Me Tarzan, You Jewel is the perfect way to heat up during the long, cold winter season." ~ *Sarah for A Romance Review*

"...a very intense book..." ~ *Tewanda for Sizzling Romances*

Titania Ladley

Me Tarzan

You Jewel

ELLORA'S CAVE
ROMANTICA PUBLISHING

An Ellora's Cave Romantica Publication

www.ellorascave.com

Me Tarzan, You Jewel

ISBN # 1419952250
ALL RIGHTS RESERVED.
Me Tarzan, You Jewel Copyright© 2005 Titania Ladley
Edited by: Briana St. James
Cover art by: Christine Clavel

Electronic book Publication: January, 2005
Trade paperback Publication: July, 2005

Warning:

The following material contains graphic sexual content meant for mature readers. *Me Tarzan, You Jewel* has been rated *E-rotic* by a minimum of three independent reviewers.

Ellora's Cave Publishing offers three levels of Romantica™ reading entertainment: S (S-ensuous), E (E-rotic), and X (X-treme).

S-*ensuous* love scenes are explicit and leave nothing to the imagination.

E-*rotic* love scenes are explicit, leave nothing to the imagination, and are high in volume per the overall word count. In addition, some E-rated titles might contain fantasy material that some readers find objectionable, such as bondage, submission, same sex encounters, forced seductions, etc. E-rated titles are the most graphic titles we carry; it is common, for instance, for an author to use words such as "fucking", "cock", "pussy", etc., within their work of literature.

X-*treme* titles differ from E-rated titles only in plot premise and storyline execution. Unlike E-rated titles, stories designated with the letter X tend to contain controversial subject matter not for the faint of heart.

Also by Titania Ladley:

Jennie In a Bottle
Moonlite Mirage
Spell of the Chameleon
A Wanton's Thief
You've Got Irish Male

Me Tarzan, You Jewel

Trademarks Acknowledgement

The author acknowledges the trademarked status and trademark owners of the following wordmarks mentioned in this work of fiction:

Tarzan: Edgar Rice Burroughs, Inc. Corporation

Chapter One

The buzz of the doorbell brought him to full awareness. Vince Santiago groaned and threw an arm across his brow. What right did anyone have to interrupt such bliss? he thought. Tucked into the curve of his body lay a voluptuous brunette...what was her name? Lucy...or Lacy? Behind him, with her small but tasty breasts pressed against his back, snuggled Katy...or was it Candy?

He mentally shrugged. What difference did it make? Who the hell cared what their names were? He inhaled a long breath full of expensive perfume mixed dangerously with the wild scent of pussy.

Ah, what a life he led!

He startled, stirring the women, when a round of sharp raps on the apartment door interrupted his thoughts.

"I'm coming, damn it!" With a sigh, he added, "Geez."

Gently untangling the various limbs from his person, Vince climbed off the foot of the bed. He glanced back at the pair and, in that one brief instant, his breath caught with a sudden slice to his heart. In slumber, the two cuddled together and let out soft moans of sleepy pleasure. Any red-blooded man would agree they made the perfect picture. Yet an image of *her* there in his bed flickered through his mind, making his pulse thud with a strange mixture of want and anger.

He shook his head. *Nope, Vince, you're not going to ruin this fantasy. It's been four freaking years. You never loved her anyway, so why the hell the sudden memory of her? Why the hell the flood of emotions?*

Narrowing his eyes on the slumbering angels, he forced himself to study the long, tanned limbs entwined like relentless vines. Clouds of straight, midnight hair melded with bright blonde waves. Curves fit into curves, interlocking in puzzle fashion. Warm, naked flesh merged together, welcoming, beckoning him. Their scent of female arousal buried beneath quiet contentment wafted up to him from his own skin. He rejoiced in the faintest stirring in his loins, and he focused on it, determined to banish this sick, unexpected obsession with a woman from his past he thought he'd forgotten long ago.

And he'd be a fool to cut this wild, hedonistic weekend short because of one stubborn woman who'd walked out on him years ago without so much as a single word of explanation.

Oh, yeah. It was time to bury *her* forever. So he'd christen that vow by getting rid of the rude son of a bitch pounding on his door. Then he'd crawl right back in bed between sugar and spice.

He grinned, already feeling better. Throwing back his shoulders, he started for the living room. But something caught his eye. He slanted a look up and chuckled. Now, how had *that* gotten there? he mused. A silky red thong dangled from the light fixture of the ceiling fan. Another glance about the room revealed half a dozen empty bottles of beer on the bedside table, and two long-stemmed wineglasses, one marked with pink lipstick, the other with red. Somewhere in the mix, a thick black candle towered above the clutter, its dark, seductive scent traveling to him on a plume of smoke. The flame persevered, but it danced and quivered, threatening to extinguish itself.

The fire suddenly split in two, three then four parts. His eyes crossed as he shook his head.

Come, Vince Santiago. Come to me!

The seductive voice echoed in his mind. He jerked his gaze back to the pair in his bed. Unless one of them had been talking in their sleep, it hadn't come from them. So then, where?

Chuckling, he raked a hand through his short-cropped hair. "Get a real grip, pal. Get a real one."

He stepped toward the door, but splashes of sexy debris littered his path. Beside his bare feet, a trail of clothing led from the bedroom door back to the bed. Vince stroked his heavily whiskered jaw. The garment heaps only contained silks and tiny feminine blouses and skirts. Where the hell were *his* clothes? He let out a smug snort and recalled last night's escapades. They had him half naked before they'd even entered the apartment. Who knew? he thought with a shrug. The elevator probably contained a tie, a shirt—hell, probably his trousers and briefs too.

He spied a pair of boxers on a nearby chair and snatched them up. With quick jerks, he jammed them on and moved out into the living room of his posh, high-rise bachelor's pad. As he neared, another knock sounded at the door and he winced.

"Jesus." Damn, his head throbbed. The sharp rap sliced through to the core of his eyeballs, right down into his shoulder blades. He kneaded the back of his stiff neck with a groan. "I said I'm coming. Quit with the fucking drum, would you?"

Yanking open the door, he stared out into the empty hall. Leaning out, he peered first to the left, then to the right. The long corridor, its plush, velvety blue carpeting spotless, sprawled still and empty before him.

"Fuck me." He ground his teeth together. What kind of sick joke was this, to interrupt his heaven for nothing?

Vince. Vince. Vince.

"What?"

But something on the floor drew his attention, had him halting his planned retreat and subsequent slamming of the door. Slowly, his gaze fell downward toward his feet.

Then he saw it.

The bottle.

As he swayed, a mesmerizing gold light winked at him, like the eye of an exotic island girl. Dizziness swam in his head. And of all things, he was getting a hard-on just looking at the bottle! He bent and scooped it up. It sat heavy and cold in his palm. Lifting his free hand, he trailed his fingertips over the outward curve of the deep purple glass, as if he caressed the flared hip of a woman. Energy zapped him, and the vase glowed in response to his touch.

Pussy. I have to have pussy now, he suddenly thought.

He shook his head. No, he'd gotten laid only an hour ago. So, why the sudden urge to screw? It made no sense. Despite his playboy pretense, he could never get it up more than once within a given twenty-four-hour period. Oh, he definitely *wanted* to, no doubt about that. There'd been a day years ago when one orgasm would be just the jump-start of his day. He let out a mental sigh, dousing the intruding memories, memories that hadn't dragged themselves up in years. He supposed his thirty-year-old body could use a dose of libido-inducing drugs every now and then.

Only this bottle seemed to be doing the trick quite nicely, he mused.

Cocking a brow, he tilted the bottle and lifted it so that he could peer through the jeweled stopper.

Come, Vince Santiago. You must come to Carnal Island.

"What in the...?" His eyes crossed and fell to the narrowed column. He'd heard the subtle message, but he'd also seen the naked body of a woman in the tiny gold-encrusted window set directly below the neck—or had he?

Aha! He knew precisely what was going on here. And understanding washed through him on a long wave of relief.

"Rex? Where the hell are you, you son of a bitch?" he said with a wry grin. He glanced up and down the hallway and waited for a long, quiet moment as the urn pulsed in his hand. But his prankster of a buddy appeared to be nowhere in sight.

Open me. Open me. Open me.

With the tip of his pinky finger, he dug into his left ear. Had he heard that, or were age and stress playing tricks on his hearing, too?

Open me. Open me now!

Yes, he'd heard it all right. There was no fighting the pull, the seductive temptation as the sweet sultry voice chanted in his head. There must be a recorded voice box or something inside, he determined silently. With a lift of his shoulders, he gripped the thick stopper and pulled against the suction.

Pop!

A salt-scented wind whipped up and around him. Vince stumbled backward and fell against the doorjamb. His vision blurred, and every wall, every elegant picture in the corridor distorted until he could no longer tell where one line ended and another began. With a deep inhalation, he caught the sweet scent of hibiscus and oranges...and woman.

Blessed, easy desire slammed into him, and at that very moment, a beautiful raven-haired female in a barely-there, pale blue, chiffon costume appeared before him. He pitched forward, fighting the drunken sensations that assaulted him. His surroundings spun around him, yet the woman remained steady as she floated slightly above him.

"Vince. Vince Santiago," she purred.

He couldn't help but blink. The carnal tone of her voice laced with the odd yet thrilling accent, zipped straight to his balls as they drew up in delight.

"You're quite the rogue, aren't you?" Her rich hair fluttered in the breeze that stirred in the corridor.

"Rogue?" Vince swallowed against the croak in his voice. "What?" He waited, but she merely levitated, studying him knowingly with those whiskey-colored eyes. "Who the hell are you?"

It was a throaty chuckle she offered, a song of honey over sand. "I'm Jennie. You just released your genie from the bottle."

His face scrunched. In the distance, he thought he heard sea gulls cawing and the swishing tempo of the surf. And he damn well knew there were no beaches in Denver.

"Jennie—in a bottle?" And it suddenly hit him. He was having a goddamn dream! He threw his head back and roared at his own stupidity. "*Oh.* Gotcha. You're my genie. Three wishes, huh? Well, for starters..." he said, sliding a look over her rounded bosom and deep cleavage. "I sure wish you'd join me and Katy...or Lacy—or whoever they are—in my bed. I think I just might be able to get it up one more time."

She rolled her eyes and hovered closer so that her gaze leveled with his. He caught the subtle scent of hibiscus and coconut entwined with warm woman. In rapid delight, his pulse leaped and his boxers grew taut over his crotch.

"Oh, give me strength, Xanthian queen, but he's a cocky one." A bored, disconcerting expression draped her lovely face.

"Hey, cut the insults, babe," he retorted, jamming his hands onto his hips. "This is *my* dream, right?"

She cupped his jaw and the heat from her touch zapped his energy. His heart rate decelerated, his spinning head slowed and his libido relaxed into a less urgent state of need.

"No, this is your sorry life, Vince Santiago, and it's time to do something about it." Her gaze rose and she narrowed her eyes like a spitting cat, focusing on a spot somewhere high in the sculpted ceiling. "Luke, honey, you picked a real winner here."

He attempted to back away and dislodge her hand from his face, but it was as if, even with the gentle contact, she had a hidden strength he couldn't overcome. Shaking his head vigorously against her palm, he growled,

"Sweetheart, there ain't nobody here by the name of Luke. And my life isn't sorry. It's perfect. It's...it's fun and..."

Her eyes darted back to stake him against the doorjamb. "Lonely?"

The suggestion instantly combusted his blood and reignited the latent ire that always stayed locked in the empty abyss most people called a heart. "That's a fucking lie. I've got every woman in the city making the rounds through my bed. How in the hell could I be lonely?"

"You've been looking for love." Her eyes stared deep and steady into his, warming him with kind yet firm affection. He couldn't look away. The genie of his dreams, it seemed, possessed a strength that far surpassed that of his slumbering, stupid ass. Inhaling sharply, he delayed a response to her accusation. Okay, add an electrifying aura and delicious, enticing aroma to that strength, he reluctantly surmised. Her fragrance filled him so completely he could almost taste her.

But her words were easily denied.

He snorted with derision. "Love?" Vince shivered. "No, thank you. I got all I need right here," he drawled, and cupped his now soft cock. "The ladies love it and I love giving it to them—but I don't *love* anyone, and I never will. You can count on that, Jennie in a bottle."

Her full lips twitched mockingly. "Is that your final word?"

"Yes, goddamn it. Now I'm ready to wake up. If you're not gonna grant me any wishes, then get the hell out of my dream. And my life, by the way, is just fine the way it is."

She sighed, a long drawn-out tune of wariness. Her hand slowly fell away from his face and the calm energy drained away along with it. "Then you leave me no choice."

"Choice? Who said anything about *me* giving *you* any choices?" He started to turn, but his feet seemed to be glued to the floor. Glancing down, he saw that they were bare, no surprise since he'd just come from his bed. But what lay sprawled beneath his feet perplexed him. The luxurious hallway carpeting had been replaced by gritty, white...*sand*? A balmy, grainy wetness cradled the soles of his feet. The tang of salty sea and exotic flowers slowly filled his nostrils, overriding the conglomeration of aromas in the apartment behind him. Inch by inch, his naked back warmed as if the sun had emerged and bathed him with its hot rays.

He jerked his gaze up and nearly buckled to his knees at the sight that met his eyes. Jennie now floated nude above him, a brilliant blue sky behind her. He battled the drugging dizziness that rekindled in his head. A rush of fear and excitement filled him. Gold dust twinkled around her, and she threw her head back chanting in some odd language he'd never heard before. Her body glowed in absolute perfection. It tempted him beyond anything Adam must have endured. This Eve held her fingertips over tight nipples as energy swirled around her. And her words became familiar, clear.

"Carnality be ever the goal of your Goddess, yet many more factors this man cannot guess." Yellow beams shot from her breasts and electrocuted Vince with painful yet blissful power. They held him by the eyes. He couldn't look away if his life solely depended on it. But he didn't want to, even though it was fascinating and somewhat disconcerting at the same time.

But despite the awe of it, an odd sense of foreboding suddenly stabbed him in the gut. "What is this all—?"

Her voice, a force of sexuality and female power, cut him off. "To Carnal Island I take him, one, two, three, four," she sang, and her arms shot upward. Her smooth body glimmered with tempting jewels and glistening skin that Vince itched to touch. "Away from the lure of this ho-hum and bore. Lead him, oh Xanthian powers that be," she now roared as winds whipped and tossed her raven hair, "to a life and a love and a woman by the sea!"

"A woman? But—" Then Vince did fall to his knees. A crack, followed by a sickening suction noise, filled his ears. He fought against a force that pulled him and sapped him of every ounce of strength. The sounds of sea gulls and surf and a tumultuous breeze intensified, tumbling around him. Citrus flavors burst in his mouth. The heat of the sun baked him while the coolness of water soothed him.

And with one final indrawn breath, he inhaled the long-forgotten scent of a woman—a woman from his past.

He'd been plagued by thoughts of her since climbing from that bed moments ago. But suddenly afflicted with amnesia, the face and the name attached to that sweet aroma now eluded him in the dream. He slipped into a black wall of unconsciousness before he could completely unearth the buried, long-dead memory of the face of heartless betrayal.

* * * * *

Jewel Dublin came awake with a start. Her heart went from calm and sleepily serene to sudden, pounding fear in a second's time. She hadn't moved a muscle, but her eyes now stared at the pink streaks of early morning sun on the ceiling. Slowing her breathing down, she drew in a long, audible gulp. Gradually, she turned her head toward the object that she'd instantly been aware of out of the corner of her eye.

Stiff and unmoving, she surveyed the purple blotch that perched upon the old highboy in her small convent room. Narrowing her eyes, she struggled to bring it into focus. Fumbling at the bedside table, she located her glasses and jammed them on. A wine bottle? Shards of fear pricked her gut. It hadn't been there when she'd gone to bed last night, and she'd not seen it before now. Which meant someone must have slipped into her room in the middle of the night as she slept. And for some unexplainable reason, felt it necessary to place the bottle on *her* dresser.

But who? One of the Sisters? The priest? A gift, perhaps, from one of the children's parents?

Her brow suddenly creased. But hadn't she locked her door last night?

Rise, Jewel Dublin. Rise from that bed and come here to the bottle.

The voice seemed to echo in her head. She sat upright and gasped, poking her glasses further up her nose. "Who...who's there?"

Come. You must open me.

Jewel clutched the scratchy, wool blanket to her chin and jerked her gaze to the left, the right, upward.

"God? Is that you?"

Oh, God, she didn't want it to be God! *Please* don't be God. She wasn't ready, not yet.

This is not God—at least not that *God.*

She flung the covers aside and scrambled from the bed. Her eyes snapped to the bottle. Hopefully, she'd be safe here with the bed in between her and the dresser. But if she found it necessary to escape, she'd have to pass by the highboy to get to the door. Which made her suddenly feel like a trapped rat.

"Who's there, and how did you know my thoughts?" She cringed at the panic in her own voice, along with the silliness of the question. A lengthy, deafening silence followed.

"Did you hear me? I want answers right now!"

A deep timbre of what she thought was an amused chuckle, rang out.

You will not be harmed. Come here, Jewel. Come here and open the bottle.

Emphasizing the man's words, the bottle flashed and glowed a warm gold, as if a yellow light bulb had lit up inside its purple glass walls. It pulsed in heartbeat rhythm. It beckoned to her sensual and hot, bringing to mind the buff men in the magazines she had hidden beneath her mattress.

"What...what's going on? I—I don't understand," she said, even as her feet seemed to step around the bed of their own accord.

Yes. That's it. Come here. Come closer.

As she neared, a tantalizing heat enveloped her. Temptation—that oh-so forbidden devil here in the convent—overwhelmed her. Her bare feet padded across the cold, raw, wood floor. Flashes of those nude centerfold men in magazines filled her mind. Hard abs, tight rears made just for squeezing, smoldering gazes that promised fulfillment. And...soft body parts that engorged in seconds and fit within a woman's passage like the rigid piece of a puzzle. Her panties flooded with excitement, but as always, she outwardly and expertly hid her desire from the outside world. Only she knew of the throbbing that plagued her sex. Only she knew of the painful longing in her heart to be held once again, to be brought to that pinnacle of insanity.

But never again would anyone hurt her the way *he* had all those years ago.

It's time, Jewel. It's time to experience a man again, just like those in your magazines, just like those you're fantasizing about right now, just like you once had so long ago.

She halted in mid-step, the bottle mere inches from her reach. A ragged intake of breath escaped her throat. "How…how did you know…?"

Open me. Open me, and you shall see…

The stopper, poised elegantly atop the bottle, glittered seductively; it charmed and enticed much like her centerfold men. Jewel inhaled and caught a whiff of citrus and wild tropical flowers. She tipped her head and furrowed her brow. Was that a parakeet she heard chirping? No. It couldn't be. There weren't parakeets here in the hillsides of Chastity, Vermont, even if it was late June.

She rubbed her eyes beneath the glasses and glanced over at the dull-gray curtains. They partially covered the open window and fluttered on the cool morning breeze. Streaks of tangerine and coral layered across the jagged horizon, blending with the lingering gray of night. Fingers of fog hovered across the pond down by the convent's wrought iron gate. Dawn made a brilliant entrance…but was it real? Could she be dreaming?

No, it's not a dream, Jewel. It's an opportunity of a lifetime. Open me now!

Her gaze jerked back to the bottle. Well, she didn't believe a word of it. Her dreams were always vivid and alive with men and the world out there she'd been hiding from. Just because it *seemed* real didn't mean it *was* real. But since it most probably was a dream, curiosity won out. It had been a stressful week teaching at the convent, so she deserved to indulge herself and see just where this dream would take her. And she certainly deserved an exciting diversion from the melancholy moods that had been plaguing her of late. These drab walls were beginning to close in on her. Thoughts of things and emotions long buried had begun to haunt her. Oh yes, she definitely needed a distraction. She was going to open the bottle and see what this was all about, what excitement might await her and help her forget.

Jewel lifted her hand and reached for it. Energy assaulted her, making her fingers twitch and her toes curl against the cold slats of the hardwood floor. She sucked in a breath and snatched her hand back.

It's okay. It won't hurt you.

Gathering a lungful of courage, she nodded her understanding. Stretching out her hand again, she gripped the narrow neck. Her body convulsed almost violently. The tempting borders of ecstasy reached for her. Heat wrapped with the luscious, just-out-of-reach edges of orgasm taunted her. She moaned and threw her head back. With a trembling grasp, she slowly drew the bottle toward her until she could cradle it against her chest. On a sigh, she closed her eyes and soaked in the warmth and passion of it. Her legs trembled beneath her long, cotton nightgown. The bottle pulsed in her hands and sent ripples of fire through her, hardening her nipples, oozing down into her womb.

And with impulsive speed, she clutched the jeweled stopper in her palm and yanked it from the bottle's neck.

Pop!

A humid breeze spun around her, plastering her high-necked gown to her body. Her loose hair blew back from her face, fluttering madly behind her. The morning Vermont chill fled her flesh and became replaced by soaking, blessed sunrays. She drew in a breath and salty sea-scents filled her lungs. Looking down, she wiggled her toes against the soft grains of warm, wet...sand?

"Hello."

The voice, no longer an echo, brought her head up with a snap. And there before her levitated the epitome of every centerfold model all wrapped up into one finely honed man. Sun-streaked, golden, long hair framed a handsome face with the most interesting aqua eyes she'd ever seen. He floated nearer and she caught the rugged, earthy scent of him. As he moved, so did his short garment, a strange rendition of a Greek god or a Roman gladiator. It revealed well-defined, powerful legs just made for...

"Jewel Dublin, it's time to change your life."

"What...who are you?"

The gentle smile he gave her momentarily distracted her from the wonder of this strange morning. "I'm Luke. And I'm your genie, here to assist you."

She raised one skeptical brow. A *genie*? Why, that was ridiculous! There was no such thing in God's universe.

"Is too."

23

With a blink at his blunt rebuttal, she wondered if she'd spoken her thoughts on genies out loud.

Jewel shifted her stance, absently noting the soft give of the sand beneath her feet. "And how would you know what's good for me and my life?"

"Well...by the same token, how would I know about the magazines?" he asked without missing a beat. He crossed his arms over his thick chest, emphasizing muscles that bulged and flexed.

She slammed the bottle onto the dresser surface with a thud. "That is none of your god—none of your business!"

The man chuckled and revealed straight white teeth within a wide, arrogant mouth. But his laughter died abruptly. He zoomed forward until his eyes were level with hers. She detected a new scent, that of...?

Of woman? Yes, the cad had the smell of some woman soaked into his very skin!

"You don't want to be a nun." He announced it as if it was a fact to report on the morning news.

She shrieked and slapped a hand over her mouth.

"No need to confirm that, love. I know it's true."

"How...how did you know?" Jewel stumbled backward across the sandy floor and dropped to the bed. It squeaked beneath her weight. She held a trembling hand to her cheek as she stared in stunned disbelief at the man. *Please*, please, *don't tell Sister Thea or Sister Neoma.* Her heart pounded against her breastbone. *They'll toss me out without a stitch on my back.*

"No need to worry. My lips are sealed. And I know because I can read your mind. I've been...gifted with certain talents that you obviously cannot deny. But all in the name of love and lust," he said cheerily.

"Oh, no…" Stabbing her fingers into her medium-length tresses, she gripped the strands as if they were her only hope of sanity. "Oh, no."

"Oh, yes," he replied, gliding over to where she sat slumped on the bed. He reached out a warm hand and lifted her chin so that her eyes had no choice but to look into the sparkle of his.

"You've been a prisoner of sorts in this convent for over four years now. Without any family or friends nearby, you turned to God after your heart was broken. You saw no need for any other man, so you devoted your heart and your time to Him, to the nuns and their school. You're a wonderful teacher to all those little ones, but that's as far as you should go, love. Don't you see? Your valiant plan to be a nun would take a commitment your fiery soul cannot fulfill. Deep down, your impetuous heart always thumped, always fought to beat. Don't be ashamed that you desire exactly what God gave you, passion and carnal needs in order to carry on and keep His world thriving. Jewel," he said huskily, tweaking her nose, "you must follow your heart, let it mend, let it be you. God will not blame you."

When she tried to lower her eyes, he once again tipped her face up to meet his stare.

"No…" Jewel shook her head emphatically. But he held her jaw and refused to hear any refusal. "Why have you come? What is this all about?"

"I told you," he said with a devastating smile that made her pulse flutter. "It's time to change your life."

"But—"

He didn't allow her to speak again. His apparition spun upward in a funnel-like swirl, then reappeared whole above her. Behind him, through the flaking ceiling and old, rotting, wooden beams, she caught glimpses of cerulean skies edged with the green fronds of palms.

And he was now naked. The sight of it took her breath away. It was as if the pages of her magazines had come to life, an Adonis, a perfectly sculpted man no longer made of one-dimensional ink. But his sex organ wasn't soft as they all were in the magazines. It stood full and erect, his sac tight and drawn up, the veiny shaft jutting upward over his rippled abdomen. In shocking response, her panties filled with a hot, sticky wetness.

But she didn't have time to so much as mentally scold herself for such a wanton response. He threw his arms wide and lifted his head toward the heavens. In a language she didn't recognize, he sang and mumbled. But somehow, she understood every word he chanted.

"Her destiny to Carnal Island shall be, the course of this journey, one, two, three." Fire and smoke churned around him. The room seemed to wane and ebb out of her vision. A sudden renewed aroma of salt mixed with oranges and acrid smoke filled her lungs. And she could swear the flavor of coconut suddenly erupted in her mouth. Above him, the ceiling burst open with a crack, revealing a wide and full mural of vivid, blue summer skies. She heard the splash of water, the song of a cockatoo, the swish of saw palmetto in a tropical forest.

Eagerness laced with a vague trepidation filled her soul. It may be a dream, she thought, but it was going to be a wondrous one!

"Lead her, oh Xanthian powers that be," he sang, "to a life and a love and a man by the sea."

The words caught her off guard. "But wait. I don't want another man to—"

But it was too late. A painful wheeze wrenched through her chest. The pleasant smells she'd been experiencing whooshed from her lungs. In their place came the scent of a man...a familiar man.

Dizziness engulfed her with fingers of soft, obscure memories.

And she floated into oblivion as a vision of him, trapped in her subconscious for more than four years, emerged to once again torment her heart.

Chapter Two

Was that goddamn sandpaper he had his face buried in? Vince groaned and opened one eye. Sprawled on his stomach, he could look out over the surface of the earth. He raised his head and stared in awe. Make that a white sandy beach, he thought with a mental grumble. He scanned the perimeter and noted the sand rose in ripples to a grassy area which, in turn, gave way to a thick forest of soaring palm trees and flowering undergrowth.

Swoosh.

He glanced behind him to see that a white-tipped wave arced its way toward shore — and crashed over him. Cool wetness soothed the flesh of his back and legs where the sun had apparently baked him in sleep. He leapt to his feet brushing the soggy grit of sand from his chest, arms, cheek and boxers.

"How in the hell did I get here?"

With his vision still a tad blurry, he peered out to sea. An aqua expanse of endless, rocking waves filled his gaze. Panic rose in his chest. It was definitely a long way from here to the cozy threesome he'd been participating in back in Denver. He scanned the horizon. Not a skyscraper or civilization or even a sailboat in sight. The cloudless, crisp blue sky, and the water, a stunning, immense obstacle, all seemed to mock him, to threaten his sanity with looming madness.

What was going on?

"You will be fine," the familiar feminine voice of Jennie said.

He spun around and searched the area for her. But he stood alone on the strange beach. "Where are you, damn it?"

"That's not as important as where *you* are."

He planted tight fists on his damp hips. "And can I ask where that might be?"

She giggled a melodious sound that made him think of sea sirens. "Weren't you listening when I cast my magic upon you? You're on Carnal Island."

Yes, he recalled that particular mention in her chants. "Carnal Island?" He nodded mockingly. "Oh yes. And do you mind if I ask where the hell that is?"

"Not at all. It's in the Gulf, *way* off the coast of Florida."

"Ah, well," he began with a relieved yet sarcastic sigh. "Then row me on back to the mainland and I'll be outa your hair, doll — that is, unless you wanna…?"

He felt the shove of her hand just before he stumbled into the sea. The surf hurtled over him as he landed on all fours. The swift kick to his ass that followed brought him face down against the shell-ridden seabed beneath the water.

All he could think was that he hadn't meant any disrespect, had only been lashing back at a genie who insisted on putting him on some freaking island against his will. He spit and sputtered as his head broke the surface of the water.

"Well, this is no dream. It's a fucking nightmare," he muttered sardonically as he spat the grains of salty sand and broken shells from his mouth.

"That may very well be true at times, dear Vince. Remember, though, it's entirely up to you. Now, I'll be on my way. You make yourself at home, you hear?"

"Wait!" He dragged himself up and whirled around. "Where are you? No. *No.* You can't...you can't just leave me here stranded on some strange island. All alone," he added under his breath.

Silence was interrupted only by the caw of a sea gull. The crash of the surf followed, pounding in tempo with his morning-after, hangover headache.

"Jennie?" Still, she didn't reply. "*Jennie?*"

He kicked the shallow water and stubbed his toe on a hidden rock. "Damn!" Hopping on one foot, he cradled the offending digit, wincing until the pain subsided.

That was when he heard the choking sounds, the short spurts of coughing and gut-wrenching gags.

Radar-like, he swiveled his head around and let go of his foot, plopping it back into the water. Up the beach about fifty yards, a sopping-wet lump that could only be a human body, washed ashore. The tide shoved it onto the beach, pushing and rolling its limp, soggy bulk. From where he stood, he could tell it was a woman by the obvious curves outlined through the long, soaked gown.

"Jennie." Vince couldn't help the set of his jaw or the grind of his teeth when he said her name. Nostrils flared, he kept his gaze fixed on her as he took flight. Sloshing through the edge of the surf, he waded up shore. His hands flexed, itched to close around that luscious neck of hers and demand to be returned to Denver. The woman — or genie or whatever the hell she was — *would* put him right back in bed between...what's-their-names.

As he neared, he halted abruptly, not due to the painful moans or the violent coughs and retching that tore from the woman's soul.

But due to the legs.

The sight of them drew him up and seemed to kick him directly in the gut. The great gams were stretched out in the edge of the surf all long and toned and creamy white. Normally, he didn't go for pale skin, but there was no denying that those legs, with the ugly nightgown bunched up around lean thighs, were delectable! He sucked in a breath when she dragged her knees up under her abdomen. His gaze moved helplessly to the upthrust twin globes of her rear. Kneeling on the beach, her forehead pressed to the sand, her arms clutched her stomach. She presented a most interesting picture, even though the noises she made were less than attractive gags. He couldn't see her face due to the medium-length strands of golden hair hiding it. But the smooth, gently curved ass proved to be irrefutably gorgeous. Despite being covered in high-waisted, cotton granny-panties, there was no mistaking the prize that came wrapped beneath.

Luscious, just made for squeezing and gripping, slamming up and down on a man's hardness. Speaking of which, he felt his wet trousers tighten. *Down boy. Not exactly the time, the place or the woman for that, now, is it?*

And he realized without surprise that this wasn't the exotic genie who'd put him here on this island in this odd, mixed-up dream.

His brows suddenly dipped. Why this strange woman had ended up here on the same beach as him at the same moment was a damned mystery. But he intended to find out after he got a good look at the face and breasts that went with the legs.

"Um…hello?" He dropped down on one knee and reached a hesitant hand out to her arm where her sleeve hung ripped at the shoulder seam. He caught the brief sensation of soft, moist skin just before she startled and shrugged his hand away. She remained leaning facedown, dry-retching.

"No—don't." She coughed again, slapping her hand on the packed sand. "I…I can't breathe."

Without warning, a protective surge welled up inside him. There was no rhyme or reason for it, but he gripped her shoulders and drew her up so that they kneeled in front of one another. Yanking her torso up against him, he immediately pressed her face into his bare shoulder and pounded on her back. Never mind the curves that molded to his hardened body, never mind the scents—had he smelled that fragrance somewhere before?—that wafted to his nostrils. He refused to watch a woman choke to death before his very eyes!

"There, there." Vince rapped hard and awkwardly against the long curve of her back, praying for her to quit coughing, to breathe. "Better now?"

With each whack, she jolted. Her head lolled and rolled until he heard her shriek with indignation as her body stiffened against him. A clear sign, he thought with relief, that he wouldn't be needing to perform CPR.

"Get your hands off me!" She shoved until they both fell back onto their rear ends.

And he could swear at that moment the whole universe shifted seasons and vaulted out of whack.

Something nagged at him. It proved vaguely annoying, as if a mosquito kept buzzing back in his brain for more blood, absently reminding him of its tiny, inconsequential life, its irritating existence.

Did he know this woman? He studied the wet ropes of hair plastered against the high-boned cheeks. Parted down the middle, the locks of wetted gold hair tumbled mid-length around her shoulders framing the heart-shaped face with layered wisps. She wasn't strikingly pretty at first glance, but the longer he examined her, the more interesting she became. The face, plain and void of a single drop of makeup, troubled him. Something flashed and wavered in his mind. It teetered on the tip of his memory, but it was no use. The memory fogged over, ebbed and tumbled back into his subconscious. Instead of going with the frustration of it, he continued to scrutinize her. Eyes of pale emerald stared back at him doe-like through thick, dark-rimmed glasses that slid down a faintly crooked little nose.

The small but pouty pink mouth sucked in a ragged breath when her gaze fell upon his face. He heard her mutter to herself in a husky, cough-roughened voice, "No. Please, no."

Ignoring the sudden pale wash of her face, his gaze slid lower, and briefly, he wondered why she wore a nightgown on a beach in broad daylight. He dismissed the thought and moved his perusal down past the high neck of the garment. The white, sheer fabric clung to a very voluptuous, soft body—Marilyn Monroe-like, he thought with puzzlement at his obvious interest. He normally went for the model-trim type...except for that one relationship long ago. His brows drew together as he recalled the confusion of that breakup. He'd never been attracted to someone quite the way he had been to his ex-girlfriend, all tall and cushy and borderline overweight. Despite those traits that some men balked at, there had been something about her, something so appealing that he'd forced himself to pursue women of the opposite body type ever since. When she'd walked out of his life, he'd sworn off her kind, determined to fend off anything that might remind him of her.

He groaned. *Shake it, Vince. Forget her. Take a look at what's right before your very eyes. Now, this...this might do.* Not nearly as heavy as...she had been, but still, there was something that grabbed his very soul and twisted in challenge. He took in the gown again, and though wet and revealing every curve and plane of her, he determined it definitely screamed *dowdy* from neck to ankle. Her style of clothing would obviously work much better for his grandmother, but garments could easily be remedied. Or removed.

Oh, and he could see quite clearly what she'd look like without the gown. Erect, brown nipples tipped full, melon-sized breasts. The tight knots strained against the thin cotton, calling to him, taking his breath away, while his mouth watered with a yen to sample them. A stirring warmed his cock, full-force and undeniable. She still knelt, so he couldn't see the legs anymore beneath the garment, but an image of their long, solid length still blazed in his brain. He shifted his stance, uncomfortable with this odd fascination for a woman who was far from the type he'd become accustomed to over the last four years. For Christ's sake, he thought with a chuckle of disgust, she wore a granny gown! And her face didn't even come close to the perfection of the models, strippers and actresses who frequented his bed of late.

So why then, did he feel a jolt of fire singe his loins when she seemed to be the epitome of some prim, plain, almost plump schoolmarm? You're losing it, buddy, he thought as he shook his head and looked away toward the deep sea. Distractedly, he watched as a dolphin broke the surface of the white-tipped waves. The scent of ocean life blew in coupled with the high-pitched song and dance of the dolphin. *Yes, you're losing your ever-loving mind if you take a risk and let something like that turn you on again.*

Unable to resist, he flicked his gaze back to her. Slowly, as if stunned to speechlessness, her eyes narrowed behind the lenses. Looking down at the nakedness of her own body beneath the cloth, she gasped and crossed her arms over her breasts.

"Who...are you?" He had to ask. The suspense was too much to bear. "And why have you ended up on this island with me?"

At his inquiries, her breath caught in her throat on an indrawn, sharp little squeal. And he could swear he saw a tear form in the corner of one eye. The sight of it took him aback, and an urge to yank her into his arms overwhelmed him.

But before he could react, she leapt to her feet. Spinning about, one bare heel grinding into the sand, she stalked off in a flurry of damp cloth and tossed tendrils. He watched intently, unable to ignore the seductive sway of her round rear. Shaking his head with deliberate slowness, he sighed as that mosquito nagged at him once again, annoying, relentless, determined.

Who the hell *was* she, anyway?

And why did his heart go out to this stranger who hadn't spoken hardly two words directly to him?

* * * * *

Jewel shoved the pain down deep and let the rage boil over.

The ass!

"Oh, how I'd love to slap that handsome face of his," she hissed to herself as she marched up the beach.

Swiping angrily at the tears, she searched for a place to go, to escape the leering, arrogant gaze of the man she loved—who didn't even remember her! Sure, she'd unintentionally lost a ton of weight, and she'd had to undergo slight facial reconstructive surgery after the accident. And yes, she'd changed her too-long, black-dyed hair back to its normal dark blonde shade and then had promptly whacked it off. She now wore glasses instead of contacts, and the normal mask of makeup she used to wear had been peeled away and tossed in the garbage when she'd fled from his apartment with raccoon eyes and a snotty nose. But *still*, if he'd loved her, he should have recognized her on sight. *Even* if it has been more than four years since he'd last laid that smoldering, dark gaze on her.

Jewel shivered at the thought of those eyes devouring her once full-figured frame. Glancing down at her soaked gown, she could see her curvy but firm body shape clearly—as had he, the cad! Due to all the changes, he obviously thought her someone else. Which equated to jerk in her book, because in his mind, it wasn't her, and he lusted quite openly for "another" woman. Not that she'd expected him to be celibate as she had been all this time. But if she could have, she would have lopped off his...privates to keep any other woman from having him after she'd dumped him.

She groaned. Oh, the humiliation, the shame, the *pain*. All those years of pining after him, remembering what she *thought* they'd had before the breakup, of trying to put him behind her, yet subconsciously watching for him in every man she saw. And at the very same time, convincing herself she'd forgotten him. It had been the reason she'd finally packed up after the big blowup, and subsequently her horrible accident, and moved from Denver, all the way out to the serene woods of Vermont. She'd holed herself up in a convent, for crying out loud, and had sworn to become a nun, simply to burn him from her memory, from her flesh and from her entire life.

And he didn't even remember her.

Well, she thought as she rounded a bend in the shoreline, she'd show him. She'd make him pay for forgetting her, for not even instinctually recognizing her on sight. How, she didn't know just yet, but it would come to her, Jewel thought with rabid satisfaction. If she had to spend one more minute with the son of a...well, she'd think of something.

She could still smell him on her. Her eyes had been shut—she hadn't even realized it was him when he'd nearly beaten her to death while she choked. But her olfactory nerves had soon kicked in, sensing that unique aroma that could only be Vince Santiago's. Her hearing had perked up, betraying her determination to remain immune to him, protesting yet soaking in every note of that deep, reverent voice of his. Heat washed over her face at the memory of being in his arms again. Her nipples had hardened instantaneously, and with mortification, she'd realized her panty briefs were becoming soaked with her own juices, adding irritatingly to the already soggy fabric. That spot between her legs, still throbbing relentlessly at the assault of his nearness, had awakened with a vengeance. That's when she'd shoved him away. The indignation of it, just the thought of her body taking on a life of its own, so very traitorous where that man was concerned, set her panties all in a wad.

She'd thought he'd have recognized her as soon as she'd broken out of that rough attempt at lifesaving or awkward comforting, or whatever he'd been trying to do to her. As soon as his gaze had fallen on her, she'd been certain he'd be suddenly demanding to know why all the changes, and why she was here in this strange place with him. Had she really changed that much that the man who'd known her inside and out didn't even recognize her anymore?

No, she thought, her teeth grinding together. The arrogant jerk had simply forgotten her, discarded all memories and references to her right out the window of his ritzy, high-rise condo.

The pad of footsteps behind her had her whirling around. And there he stood, that wide, sculpted, bare chest puffing and falling with excitement, as if he were her hunter and she his prey. His boxer shorts were drenched so that she could see every curve, every smooth line of his manhood outlined to huge perfection. Her breath quickened and she jerked her gaze back to his face. Quite the mistake given the fact it had the power to devastate her just as much as his sex did.

She fidgeted under his sharp scrutiny, the chocolate eyes probing her with that infamous, sweet power — power to melt female guts in one single glance. The black slash of one brow rose while the other dipped, and he puffed out his cheeks on a sigh. She could well remember the feel of that stubbled jaw beneath her palms, the touch of her thumbs against his wide, wet mouth as she held his face in her hands right before the slam of a desperate kiss. He sniffed nonchalantly as she stared at him, the nostrils of his straight, perfect, manly nose flaring. Her gaze fell to the cleft in his chin...oh, how she longed to dip her tongue in it again, to kiss it, to explore it with her fingertips!

"Are you all right?"

Am I all right? she thought sarcastically. Jewel snorted out loud, relieved that the tears were, even now as her heart lurched with agony, drying on her cheeks. "Quite."

Again, he didn't make any indication of recognizing her. Sure, her voice didn't sound nearly the same as it had years ago. It was now extremely raspy from all that choking and coughing. And she'd only spoken a handful of words so far, but still, it rankled her to no end that he could look at her, hear her, hold her and not know who she was.

"Are you sure?"

"Sure."

He sighed and raked a hand through his short-cropped, jet-black hair, just the way he always had. "Okay, so we've—or rather, I've—established that you're going to live. So. What now?" He folded his arms over that A-plus, male model chest of his. A slow tumble of liquid heat rolled through her veins, making her tremble with the need to touch those pectorals. God, to experience the curved hardness of them in her palms once again! As if in taunting reply, the sun just then peeped from behind a cloud and bathed him in white rays, making him all the more appealing as his eyes twinkled with mockery.

She wasn't going to speak. She wasn't. Stubbornly, she crossed her arms over her chest, too, though partially to hide his prying eyes from her double-crossing, rock-hard nipples.

"Ah." He pursed his lips and clucked his tongue. Angling his head, he glanced up at the fronds of a palm tree that began to dance as the wind picked up. "So you're going to either communicate with me in one-word, guttural sentences, or not speak to me at all. Is that the way it's going to be while we're here, obviously stranded on this damn island together for who knows how long?"

A sea gull cawed, taking flight out and across the waves. The water seemed to be gradually rising and tossing in a turbulent rush. The scent of coconut mingled with the manly aroma of him, swirled around her. All proof he spoke the truth. They were definitely on an island together, though that didn't mean they were alone, and it certainly didn't mean they were stranded.

She fisted her hands where they remained entangled in her folded arms and finally croaked, "Yes."

The easy nod he gave her belied the annoyance and slight fury that suddenly blazed in his eyes. "You got a name?"

A name? Oh, yeah, I got a name, and you damn well know what it is!

When she only speared him with a loathing stare, he replied, "I'm Vince. Vince Santiago." He stepped forward and thrust his hand toward her, daring her to take it in hers. "I'm a broker from Denver. Finance, real estate, that sort of thing."

Yes, she knew exactly what and who he was. Helplessly, she looked down at the familiar, large hand suspended too near to her abdomen. Memories assailed her of those long fingers expertly strumming her nipples and her clit, sinking inside her with devastating bliss. The mere thought of it nearly brought her to her knees, right to the brink of ecstasy. Her breasts tingled with insistent demand and that spot between her thighs pounded like the surf behind her. But, as always, she controlled her breathing and her facial expressions and glanced back up at his egotistical expression. He continued to hold the hand out, determined to get a pleased-to-meet-you-for-the-first-time handshake from her.

Okay, she thought, get it over with. Then move on, go look for this Luke genie guy, then get back to the convent...and boredom.

"Jew—uh, I...I'm Jane." She finally released her hand from beneath her elbow and extended it to him.

He sliced a look at her tight, balled fingers. "Um, you can open your fist now."

She obeyed, though she hadn't a clue why. She supposed it was that persuasive, suave tone he'd perfected long ago. His hand slid into hers as soon as she uncurled her fingers. He gripped her with warmth and strength and a sexual squeeze that pumped her system with another wave of throbbing need. It traveled with lightning-quick speed from his hand, up her arm and straight down to her womb. Though she was a tall, big-boned woman herself, his hand dwarfed hers making her feel a femininity she hadn't felt in years. Jewel inhaled, fighting the pleasant sensation of that long-awaited skin-to-skin contact.

"You can open your eyes now."

Her eyelids flew open on a humiliated gasp. She yanked her hand from his and stumbled back. Lord, she hadn't realized the sensation of simply holding his hand would render her transfixed. It mortified her beyond acceptance that he had such effortless power over her.

"I...I...I'm sorry."

He merely grinned a smug, satisfied grin that instantly doused her fire. "Not a problem. Not a problem at all."

Jewel couldn't take it a moment longer. She had to get away from him. The torture, the conglomeration of both desire and irritation at his conceit were too much to bear. With her eyes glued to his, she backed several steps away. Then she tore her gaze from his and turned tail and ran.

"Jane! Where the hell—Christ," she heard him swear as she veered inland into the undergrowth of foliage. Despite the intermittent foot and shin pain of tripping over sharp saw palmetto fronds and fallen limbs, she trudged on. Her ankle suddenly burned, but she ignored the wetness—was it blood or sweat?—as it dribbled down over her foot. She had to get away, get far, far away from him. There was no other way about it. Unless she wanted to leave her heart wide open for him to take another stab at her. And that wasn't happening again in her lifetime or his, not while *she's* in charge of her own life.

A sudden chilly breeze blew in stirring the thick Spanish moss strung overhead in the scattered trees. The scent of rain—or was it the aroma of winter?—clung to the air, filling her lungs with the omen of bad weather. The late-morning sky darkened as puffs of gray clouds moved in. She glanced around, frantic for somewhere to hide from the coming storm, from him. Moving clumsily through the halophytes of the mangrove, she skirted a cluster of pine flatwoods and a dense understory of gumbo-limbo. She wasn't sure what tropical area she'd appeared in after that encounter with the wine bottle on her convent dresser, but Jewel knew her foliage well. Educated as a schoolteacher, she'd often taken her Science students deep into the textbook studies of the various species of plant and animal life worldwide. Jewel was very familiar with the colors and characteristics of the crab wood, pigeon plum and soldier wood, and she now knew them on sight as she weaved her way through the forest, escaping those eyes, those hands. The frenzied chirps of birds caught her attention and she halted her steps, planting her hand on the rough, jagged bark of a palm tree to catch her breath for a moment. Above, a colorful cluster of cockatoos and parakeets took flight as a frosty gust of wind whipped the treetops.

And that was when she saw it. There, fluttering down through the tangled limbs of the forest ceiling, snowflakes fell. Large, white particles of snow blew through the swaying limbs, spewed from the bowels of the dark clouds overhead.

"Snow? In the tropics?" She couldn't help but croak it out loud. The sight of it, along with the white-puffed condensation of her own breath, stunned her into a catatonic state.

"I'll be goddamned."

She jerked her gaze down to find Vince standing right behind her. He stared up at the falling flakes, his hands planted on narrow hips. She watched, mesmerized, as the snow rained onto his handsome, upturned face. That naked chest rose and fell, his breath puffed out in plumes of white and she thought of a dragon, prepared to breathe his wrathful fire. A thrill went through her, warming her skin so that the sudden, below-freezing temperatures that surrounded her, heated to boiling. She dragged her perusal from those hardened nipples of his, remembering with crystal-clear clarity the tightness of them on her tongue, the salty taste of them. She rolled her fingertips together, almost feeling one of his taut areolas between her fingertips. The swift memory of them abrading over her own nipples drew a whimper from her pursed lips, and she tightened her thighs together as a gush of stickiness filled her crotch.

"It's fucking snowing," he groaned. "What the *hell* is going on here?"

* * * * *

She knew their protégés couldn't see or hear her, so Jennie Sebastian Slayton shrieked with delight and spun in a circle. Suspended above the island where the couple stood in the forest below, Luke at her side, she fell into his arms and giggled.

"I just love snow, don't you?"

Luke never failed to give her libido a charge. His aqua eyes bathed her with lust and eternal love, even as he shivered with the biting cold. "Uh, no. It's why I moved from Denver to Florida to start my business all those years ago."

She pinched his cheek. He flinched, but she growled with satisfaction when his hot hand slid down to cup the cheek of her ass. "Come on, master. Get in the spirit."

"I'll get in the spirit, all right," he warned, sliding his other hand into the deep vee of her toga dress.

Jennie moaned and her head fell back when he shoved aside the sheer fabric and claimed an already hard nipple. He sucked it into his mouth and played havoc on the very tip with his scalding-hot tongue. She could smell the swift scent of their mixed arousals. Carnal heat engulfed every cell of her immortal body. Luke could never fail with her, she thought on a pant. And the dampness that flooded her pussy only reaffirmed that.

But she had a job to do.

With a discipline she was still learning to control, she yanked his head from her breast with a resounding *pop*.

"What?" His dilated pupils nearly wiped out the entire circle of the blue of the irises. And at that moment, with his lips all moist, his eyes glazed with passion and his hardened *phallus* pressing into her abdomen, she thanked the gods that she'd been banished to that bottle all those centuries ago. It had been a long, lonely journey, but it had led her here, to reign over Earth's Carnal Island, to have purpose and meaning in her eternal life. And it had led her to this man whom she loved so very much, that it almost frightened her at times.

He'd been ordained immortal after her sister, the Queen of Xanthus, had removed his mortal heart and replaced it with immortality. Their love for one another had sustained them, brought them together forever and placed them back here on Luke's Carnal Island to complete an ongoing mission. As the God and Goddess of Carnality, she and Luke would handpick and choose Earthlings, and summon them to the resort. They would guide and teach them about the importance of nurturing carnal needs, something essential in the makings of their final goal. Everlasting love.

"What?" he asked again, crouching slightly to grind his thick rod against the sticky lips of her *nymphae*.

"Remember our job here?"

He blinked and slid a reluctant glance down at the couple arguing below them. "Oh, yeah. Carnality, love and all that."

"All that?" She stepped away from him, immediately feeling the biting cold rush between their bodies. "Luke

Slayton, are you already tiring of your honorable position of God of Carnality of the Xanthian realm?"

His eyebrows slanted down in a large U. "Of course not. It's just that…" He shifted his stance and reached for her hand, sucking her index finger between his lips. She nearly buckled right then and there at his feet, but complete devotion to her cause had her merely biting her lip when he nipped at her fingertip.

"Well, you see…" he went on, dragging the pad of his tongue across her palm so that her breath clogged and tumbled straight into her cunt. "I can't think when you're around. I want you. I need you." He kissed her wrist, then her inner forearm, and stars twinkled behind her eyelids as they fluttered shut. "I love you and I want to fuck you again."

She whimpered. "But we just made love an hour ago, master, right before we went to seek them out."

He yanked her into his arms. Heat engulfed her once again, and she sighed at the contentment that soaked her soul.

"And we're going to do it again"—he kissed her, drawing her bottom lip in between his teeth—"and again" —he reached down and cupped her ass — "and again." One hand stabbed into the hair at her nape and he slammed her mouth tight against his. His lips covered her protesting, tight mouth. She struggled to ignore the wine-flavored taste of his kiss, the expert sweep of his tongue, the musky scent of him. And the tempting grind of his tool against her wet sex lips.

Power, she silently coaxed herself. She must use power and restraint to keep herself, and even Luke, on the right path they'd been gifted with. "Luke..." she panted against his mouth.

"What, love." It came out ragged, desperate, and it made it all the harder for her to toss up her hand and throw up a protective wall of magic between them.

He pressed his hands against the invisible wall. "What d'ya do that for?"

She righted her clothing and smoothed her hair. "Look, just take a look." With a trembling hand that itched to touch Luke once again, she pointed down at the couple. They shivered in the snowstorm as they flung their arms up at one another while in the midst of a heated conversation. Their voices carried boisterously on the wind, while the green of the tropical ground quickly turned to white around them.

"They need us," Jennie said with a sad tone. "It's what we're here for. It's why I conjured up the snow in the first place. Please, Luke. We must help them *before* we...help ourselves."

He sighed and flashed her a smile that devastated her almost as much as his kiss had. "You're right. My old college buddy always did need help when it came to women." With a clearing of the throat and a quick adjustment of his crotch, he asked, "But how does the snow figure in, babe?"

Joy filled her heart at his approval. Almost automatically, she flicked her hand and dissolved of the wall. Throwing her arms around his neck, she purred, "Because, my lover, she's obviously avoiding him, and he's struggling with his attraction to her. What a better way to bring about our goal than to force them to survive together, to make them seek out one another's body heat and assistance in order to stay alive. Get it?"

His eyes shone a potent mixture of pride, passion and love. He gathered her closer. "You know what, Goddess?"

"What, God?"

"I'm a lucky man to be strapped to the likes of one meddling, brilliant, hot genie for eternity."

She squealed with satisfaction and smacked a kiss on his stunned mouth. "And I'm a lucky woman to have the likes of one horny, handsome, good-hearted genie for eternity."

He smacked her ass. "Hot damn! Let's get started and teach those two the importance of lust."

"And love," she added with a note of sternness.

"And love," he returned softly, cradling her in his arms with a tenderness that had nothing to do with fornication and everything to do with just that.

Love.

Chapter Three

If it wasn't for the twisted sort of erotic picture she presented, Vince would have choked her. This woman, whoever the hell she was, was the most stubborn, bull-headed chick he'd ever encountered. She'd rejected every suggestion he'd made, and obviously had no intention of staying with him for her own safety—if her awkward retreating trudge through two-foot-deep-and-rising snow was any indication.

"Jane, goddamn it!" He had to shout above the moaning, whistling winds. "Will you just get back here and listen to me?"

He watched as she spun so quickly, he feared she'd spiral right down into the sand beneath the snow. Her eyes blazed through the torrent of white, blustery weather, twin green flames amplified by the lenses of her ugly glasses. And he thought he'd never seen a more interesting woman in all of his life.

"Listen to you?" she shrieked. Flinging her arms up to emphasize each word, she roared, "Do you really think— what was it, Vince?" At his nod, she went on. "That an educated woman such as myself, would really listen to a pompous ass such as yourself, and think that my survival solely hinged on my dependence on you?"

"Well...sure." He added a hesitant shrug.

"Oh!" Said and released, he thought, with her pretty white teeth clamped as tight as a vise. He watched, fascinated, as her body shivered violently, the previously wet gown now a cone of ice around her body.

"You're still—" she started to say. "Oh, never mind." And with that, she balled her hands and started to turn. Lifting one leg, she grunted and pulled.

But apparently, her feet had become frozen in place.

Her dilemma instantly overjoyed him. Despite the frigid, rapidly dropping temperatures and involuntary trembles of his near-naked body, Vince couldn't help but chuckle. He folded his arms and rocked back onto his bare, frozen heels.

"Just *what*," she hissed, her heated gaze rising to snare him, "are you laughing at?"

He cleared his throat feigning innocence. "Uh, the snow?" He looked up into the ice-covered limbs of the trees and palm fronds. "The cockatoos frozen in the trees?" He looked everywhere but at her. "The...the bungalow? That hadn't been there a minute ago?"

"What?" She swiveled her head, her eyes narrowed like a mistrusting hyena on one of those nature-themed cable channels. Her searching gaze fell upon the tiny little gingerbread cottage tucked back into a group of flowering—but frozen—jacaranda trees. "Where did *that* come from?"

"Precisely my question." He couldn't take his eyes off the snowbound structure. It seemed to twinkle and call to him, the thick swirl of smoke that puffed from the chimney a promise of thawed feet and possible food and water. Paned windows edged with frilly curtains beckoned him to the cozy space within. Without another word, he traipsed through the drifts until he stood at the small stoop, his fist positioned to knock. Slowly, the wood-slatted door swung open with a squeak, yet he hadn't knocked or even touched the latch. Waves of heat drifted out to him, taunting and teasing, enveloping him with relief and comfort. The scent of beef stew filled his nostrils and his stomach growled in gleeful, anticipatory response. Through the open door to the far wall, he could glimpse a cozy stone fireplace crackling with the makings of a blessed fire. Above the licking flames, a black cauldron hung across an iron bar. A small table sat on one side, a quilt-laden bed on the other.

"Hello? Anyone home?" But for the crackle of the fire, silence met his ears. Though it appeared to be a well-used abode, not a soul emerged to greet him. Maybe they'd gone out hunting and wouldn't mind temporary guests? Or maybe this was Jennie's doing, a more probable scenario given the fact the home appeared equipped for cold weather rather than the tropics. What she was up to, he hadn't a clue, but the fact of the matter was, they needed shelter—and *now*, he determined, thinking of Jane's frozen, shivering body in the woods behind him.

"Well?" she shouted, her voice echoing across the thicket. "Are you just going to stand there staring inside?"

So transfixed with his thoughts, he almost didn't hear her. Turning, he saw her across the tiny clearing, her feet still frozen where she stood. He chuckled to himself. Any other man might march right in and slam the door in her face, ending the snarling comments and scathing anger that, for some unknown reason, boiled within her.

But not Vince Santiago. He might be a learned playboy of late, but he never lost respect for women. Determined, he took the few steps in stride and entered the bungalow. Pleasant heat and the scent of the stew mixed with sugar and cedar filled his lungs. Immediately, his bare feet soaked in the warmth of the floor, melting the blood within and bringing the toes back to life.

"You son of a bitch. Go ahead. Leave me here to freeze to death. I'll haunt you, Vince Santiago. I swear, I'll haunt you after I die!"

Vaguely, he heard her rough, raspy voice, the cursed promise carrying out across the forest. But he had to locate some water before he addressed that comment. Swinging his gaze from left to right, he wasn't surprised to find the large bottle of water sitting upon the table. He strode quickly to it. Lifting it, he twisted off the top and doused his wrist, as a mother might her baby's bottle.

Ah. Warm, just as he suspected it would be. He reapplied the lid and went directly out the door, down the few stairs and through the deep snow. His feet almost sizzled in protest to the reintroduction of cold, but he ignored it, knowing he must first free her then seek relief for them both.

"What are you doing?"

Her wary tone struck an odd chord in his heart. He looked up at her, and once again, the nagging familiarity assaulted him. Had he seen her somewhere before? No, it couldn't be. He remembered all women, and especially those who made an impression on him such as this one did.

"I'm going to get your damn feet out of the ice and snow so you won't be able to haunt me. That is, unless you object like you do with everything else." Vince twisted off the bottle's cap.

"You're...you're—really?" The relief and faint tone of appreciation in her voice touched him somehow, giving him the hint of hope at getting through the day with this surly woman.

"Yes, really." First, he poured a drop or two here and there to avoid shocking her skin. Next, he methodically doused both feet.

"Ah!" She threw her head back and sighed. Vince glanced up at her and watched, spellbound, as she closed her eyes in ecstasy. He briefly indulged himself in the vision that they were in bed and he'd just plunged himself between her thighs. But he didn't fantasize for long. Shaking the loony thought from his befuddled mind, he swept her firm, curvy body one last time with a furtive glance. The guttural, sexy moan, coupled with the hardened nipples through the frozen fabric, had brought his manhood back to life, defrosting its temporary freeze. Which wouldn't do if he had to spend another moment of agony in the company of the Ice Princess.

As if to emphasize his thought, the winds picked up in force, dumping thicker, more dense snow on them. How in the hell it could snow in the tropics was beyond him, but he suspected it had something to do with this strange dream and the miraculous appearance of the much-needed shelter. And Jennie, of course.

"Come here." He tossed the bottle into a snowdrift and reached for her.

She stiffened, words of protest poised on her lips.

"Don't argue with me, damn it. Do you want to get frostbite?" But he didn't give her time to reply. Tamping down the anger that threatened to spew forth, he snatched her up and tucked her against his chest. Ignoring the soft fan of her breath on his neck and the hesitant rise of her arms around his neck, Vince carried her into the bungalow and kicked the door shut behind him.

* * * * *

Oh, to be in his arms again!

Jewel took in the myriad of sensations, and the oven of toasty warmth that suddenly surrounded her as they entered the quaint, one-room cottage. Across the small space, the fire sputtered and sizzled, thawing her feet further. The heat that passed from his chest through her gown accelerated the overall lessening of discomfort. The numbness of her arms ebbed as she tightened her hold around his neck. Angling slightly toward his torso as he carried her, she nearly let out a cry of relief bathed by ecstasy as one breast pressed against sinewy muscles. Both nipples sprang to life, tingling, transmitting a delicious current of desire into the very depths of her core. The feel of one strong arm wrapped about her chilly back, and the other hooked under the backs of her knees, had her practically sobbing in bliss. Laced with the scents of saltwater and delicious stew, she could smell his earthy scent, could almost taste it in her watering mouth. And tucked in his wet boxers just below her rear, his penis taunted her. With the exception of the "lifesaving" embrace he'd given her on the beach less than an hour before, it'd been so very long since her pussy had been this close to his cock.

As if to reiterate that thought, the tender folds between her legs engorged with a pulsing fury, hardening her clit.

But before she had time to solidify her resolve and shake the pleasures from her system, he set her on the soft bear rug before the fire.

"Take off your clothes."

Her gaze snapped up. "Excuse me?"

"I said, take your clothes off." Nonchalantly, he swung the pot of stew out and began stirring the bubbly mixture.

Ignoring the tightening of her belly at the appetizing sight of food, she replied, "You're crazy. I'm not getting naked for you."

The look he shot her sent a diffuse rush of heat to her face. "For me? Who said it was for me?" He bent and blew on a ladleful of soup. Hesitantly, he pursed his lips and sucked in a mouthful, clucking his tongue around in his mouth with approval as he swallowed. "Mm, just right."

Goldilocks. The absurd thought popped into her mind and she let out a sarcastic snort. "So said the arrogant, mean old bear as he sampled the porridge."

One inky-black eyebrow arched sardonically. "You've been reading too many bedtime stories. Now," he said as he dropped the utensil back into the pot, "get out of that...lovely dress of yours."

The vague insult riding the slight sneer in his voice didn't go unnoticed. But she let it pass and crossed her arms over the damp nightgown. Tapping one slightly numb foot against the furry rug, she snapped back, "I will not."

"You will." His deep voice, oddly quiet and firm, filled her ears with a shiver.

He took one step toward her so that she could feel the inferno of his chest singe her breasts more headily than the blaze of the fire. Even though she stood tall herself, she had to tip her face up to meet his stare. She poked her glasses further up her nose to look straight through the lenses. His eyes bore into her, black instruments pinning her in place, leaving her no choice but to look intently back at him.

And something about that moment that passed between them, about the brief flash of hazy recognition that flashed in his eyes then faded just as quickly, assailed her with the wrath of God. He wasn't trying very hard to remember, that she was sure of. In fact, it almost appeared as if he purposely pushed the remnants of recollection aside. Pure, blatant denial is what it was, whether consciously or subconsciously, she didn't know. But, the evidence of that wrath she'd suddenly experienced seconds ago, pounded in her head in the form of lethal, carefully controlled, blessed restraint. Despite the pleasant indulgence of his nearness, she reaffirmed her decision to keep up the identity farce. Power. She had all the power here. Oh, but how it rankled her! How could he be this close to her, have held her so tenderly only moments ago, and still not know who she was?

The internal question plagued her, ate away at her gut like acid and made her all the more determined to punish him. Okay, so the irresistible attraction was still there, she admitted. But that didn't mean she had to act on it, or give him the satisfaction of revealing her identity. It was his problem not hers that he didn't remember her, and she refused to help the egotistical fool along and clear up his lame confusion. Jewel had the upper hand, whether he knew it or not. She would hold that one single trump card very closely and guard her heart with it if she had to die trying.

He set his jaw, a gesture that should have warned her far in advance. His eyes never leaving hers, he raised his hand. Before she realized what he'd intended, the sharp swish of ripping fabric filled the cabin.

Jewel gasped. She looked down in horror to see that both of her breasts bulged from the gaping slash he'd just made of her gown. Having hooked his fingers in the high neck, he'd yanked downward with a firm sweep. The row of tiny fasteners gave way, and dozens of buttons popped and went arcing across the room, tapping against the wood floor in a click-and-pop tune.

"You son of a—" She started to step back and raise her arms to cover herself, but he proved to be quicker than lightning. An animalistic fire lit his eyes, frightening yet oddly thrilling her. Both of his hands rose this time, and jerked the tattered edges down and over her shoulders. The gown had been fairly loose before its destruction, so there was no counting on it clinging to her hips in her defense as it fell. Horror-stricken, Jewel watched as the entire weighted-down garment plopped to the floor at her feet in a split second. With it went her panties, as if connected to the gown.

"How *dare* you!" Her own voice rang in her ears with pathetic desperation and vulnerability. Humiliation filled her soul, igniting a level of anger she'd never encountered before. Though removal of the cold, damp fabric from her skin, coupled with the sudden wash of heat from the fire, gave her instant relief, she bent and fumbled to grasp the gown, to pull it back up and cover herself. His hungry gaze flitted down to devour her naked flesh, and damn it, but those black-as-sin eyes burned her hotter than the fire had!

He knelt before her, and she paused without choice when he gripped her hand firmly, halting her attempt to raise the tattered cloth. "No. You will not keep the damn thing on."

"Oh! You pompous ass!" She gritted her teeth together and raised her free hand. But once again, he demonstrated his expert, reflexive power over her. He caught her arm just before her hand made contact with his cheek. Her wrist ignited with a searing fire, while her palm itched to feel the sting of contact.

"That's enough." He stood and dragged her up with him, and another brief sweep of his eyes over her hot flesh had her womanhood smoking with reluctant desire. She ignored the flood of wetness that dribbled out of her cunt. *You're an idiot for deriving any sort of pleasure from this bully.*

"You have no right to strip me naked." Oh, God, was that tears she felt stinging the backs of her eyes?

He paused, a brief, tender flicker lighting his gaze. But it was just that. Brief. "I didn't strip you naked, goddamn it!"

She snapped a look down at her own nakedness then back up to narrow her gaze on him. His own eyes had followed the same path as hers, and this time, they remained locked on her breasts as she spoke. "Look at me, damn you. At my face!" She waited until he dragged those black, dark weapons back up to look at her. "*I* didn't strip myself. And you claim you didn't strip me of my gown, so what is it, magic or something?"

The sarcasm in her voice wasn't nearly thick enough for her. And she supposed it was due to the fact that his heated gaze had fallen once again as she spoke, and currently bounced back and forth between her two taut nipples. He still held her wrists, and the sick thrill that suddenly assaulted her had her fighting to suppress a groan of pleasure. She watched as his mouth fell open in stunned silence.

But not for long. "Oh, I'm looking at you all right. And magic?" He finally lifted his stare and bathed her with eyes that brought to mind hot, thick, potent coffee. "I'm beginning to wonder..."

Lord, this was ridiculous! "Let. Me. Go." She glared at him through the thick lenses of her glasses, wishing she could conjure up some sort of evil-eye power to strike back at him through the magnification of them.

His nostrils flared as he narrowed his lids. "Not until you promise not to put the frozen gown back on."

"Oh, and what may I ask," she purred sarcastically as she struggled to no avail to free her wrists, "do you suppose I don instead?"

He jerked his jaw toward the bed. "Hell, a fucking blanket. *Anything* that's dry and warm and won't make you catch your death of cold."

Jewel halted her resistance against his hold. She blinked. "Aw, you're worried about little ol' me catching a cold?" she asked with a pouty jut of her bottom lip. And even though she continued her act of defiance, his obvious-but-brutal-way-of-showing-it concern had struck a tender chord somewhere deep inside her.

He squeezed her wrists. "I'm worried about having to nurse a stranger back to health in a remote cottage—on a possibly deserted, tropical, but snow-ridden island with no medical facilities nearby. And in a freaking nightmare I can't seem to wake up from."

Stranger. Nightmare. The two words had the effect of stabbing her right in the soul and strangling that tender chord of mere seconds ago. Which only served to make her more determined to hide her identity from him. God, how had she ever loved this man? Jewel suddenly wondered. But she had no answers. She only prayed her voice would remain deeply husky from the damage all that coughing had done to her throat. She had to get through this *nightmare* in an intact piece, and get this jerk exterminated from her heart for good before returning to Vermont.

"Let go of me and turn your back. I'll obey the master and go wrap my cold, naked, vulnerable-to-death body in a quilt. Will *that* satisfy Your Highness?"

He stared at her for a long while, as if he warred with the possibility that she had something else up her sleeve — that is, *if* she'd had a danged sleeve to put something up. Finally, he released her arms and stepped back, daring her to defy him.

Jewel sent him a haughty look as she turned and splayed her hands over her buttocks with automatic self-consciousness. Despite the mortification she felt at partially baring her backside to him as she crossed to the bed, a relentless thrill at being naked in his presence once again, swirled through her chest and settled down into the abyss of her core. There in those depths, excitement simmered with each step she took, each time her sex-lips glided back and forth over one another with the movement.

But the sensation came to a rolling boil when she heard him moan behind her. And she realized she'd forgotten to demand that he turn his back before she'd turned hers.

Or *had* she forgotten?

* * * * *

Vince hadn't been able to suppress the involuntary moan that had escaped his throat. He watched, spellbound by her perfectly shaped ass, as she tried lamely to cover herself, scramble to the bed and yank off the top blanket. With adept swiftness, she swirled it around her until she stood cocooned in its thickness, her pale but interesting face with the owlish glasses, peeping out over the patchwork fabric.

"Happy now?" she snarled, and suddenly that sour face fascinated him even more than before.

He cleared his throat and shifted his stance. Ignoring the heavy engorgement of his cock within the cold, wet boxers he wore, he replied blandly, "Ecstatic. Now get over here and finish warming yourself up. And if you happened to miss breakfast, too, and your stomach is anything like mine," he added, turning to stir the contents of the pot, "you're famished about right now. So grab a bite to eat. Never know. It could be our last."

"We're obviously in *somebody's* house, and it isn't mine or yours. I'm not so sure we should eat their food, or stay here much longer."

He'd sensed her approach even before she'd spoken. Her nearness curiously thrilled him, sending a shiver of anticipation through him. His limbs started to warm and his cock to harden. He shot a look at the bed he knew he'd share with her before this hallucination ended. Sex or not, they would share that space. Vince heard the soft scrape of wood against wood as she pulled out a chair from beneath the tiny table. Reaching for two dishes on a shelf to the right of the fireplace, he ladled up stew and turned to place the bowls on the table.

"No, I'm almost certain no one lives here. We're in a dream, doll. It's all make-believe. Now eat." He slid one bowlful of stew toward her, along with a soup spoon he'd located in a tray upon the small corner countertop.

"And if someone does live here?" She huddled in a ball inside the blanket and eyed the steaming stew with undisguised hunger. The sight of her longing for food nearly melted his heart. That protectiveness reared up inside him again, threatening to make him do impetuous things that would only cause the wedge between them to tighten if he didn't go about things right.

"Trust me on this one."

She slid him a look that said her trust in him could fit on the head of a pin.

Instead of examining her further, or that protective instinct that annoyed him to hell and back, he scanned the small kitchenette and noted a bottle of wine on ice in the one-basin sink. Had it been there when he'd first entered the bungalow? Shaking his head, he refused to examine the possibilities. This was a bizarre, crazy day he'd woken up to in his apartment in Denver. He supposed a little wine might come in handy to either clear his head, or numb his rampant thoughts of this woman whom he still couldn't quite place.

And who had the subtle power to strengthen her appeal to him by snarling words just as much as by glimpses of her bare, smooth, soft skin.

He reached for two mugs, set them on the table and unraveled the wire from around the bottle top. Twisting, he dislodged the cork and poured red wine into each of the mugs. He plucked up one cup and took a long swallow, refreshed as the sweet-tart flavor slid down his throat.

Vince sat, refilled his cup and slurped a spoonful of soup, sighing as the hot steam swirled around his nose. The flavor of chunky vegetables and hearty meat filled his mouth. He glanced across the small space of the table.

"What?"

She stared at him, her mouth hanging agog. "You...you really think it's okay? I mean, what if The Three Bears or whoever"—her eyes scanned the tiny room—"poisoned the stew?"

He dropped his spoon with a clatter against the ceramic bowl. "You can't be serious."

"You know just as well as I do that everything that's been happening since...since I—we—woke up this morning, is bizarre." She leaned over her soup, spearing him with a worried stare. "You never know what could happen in a dream like this."

Ah, so she'd resigned herself to that explanation, as well. "Yes, anything can happen. *Anything.*"

She blinked, awareness of his meaning dawning in her eyes. Through the half-inch thickness of the lenses, he thought he saw expectant, emerald fire ignite there.

But first he had to slake another kind of hunger.

"Eat. It's delicious and it's fine. No poison, see?" He shoveled a heaping spoonful into his mouth, then another. "I'm alive and well."

She looked down at the bowl and stared for a long while. Hesitant, she instead lifted the cup and drained the wine in one gulp. He immediately refilled it.

Inhaling, she picked up her spoon and blew. The sight of her pursed lips had him fantasizing about them wrapped tightly around his penis, moving up and down on his shaft and taking him in. His loins stirred, filling his cock with blood, making him ache and throb with need. And when she swallowed and sighed, her eyelids fluttering shut with bliss, he nearly came right then and there.

"Oh, this is good." Was that sincerity, distraction or sarcasm he heard in her tone?

"Yes. Scrumptious."

"So…" she said lightly, stirring until the carrots and potatoes rose to the surface in her bowl. "Have you ever been in love?"

Vince gulped, almost choking on a hunk of meat. "Excuse me?"

"Have you ever been in love before?" Obviously enjoying herself, she slurped up more stew, emptying the bowl before tipping her head back to drain the second glass of wine. "It's a simple, straightforward, easy question to answer," she said pertly, setting the mug on the table with a sharp rap.

He scraped the last of his soup up in the spoon and swallowed. Shoving the bowl away, he rose, the chair grinding on the floor behind him. "That's none of your damn business."

"Ah," she purred, lifting the bottle to pour a third cup. "Touched a chord, huh?"

What in the hell was she after? A stranger suddenly prying into his personal life? It struck him as odd, almost eerie. "No."

Jane stood abruptly, her chair crashing to the floor behind her. Strategically preventing the blanket from falling, she set her hands on either side of her place setting and leaned in toward him. But still, he caught an errant glimpse of smooth, full, round breasts. Her cloud of hair gleamed with pale highlights in the firelight as it swept forward across her shoulders, framing her heart-shaped face. Dry now, he noted how it had brightened several shades lighter. His hands flexed with a need to comb through the tresses, to be filled with the ample bosom. A sweet, painful jolt ripped through him, and his mouth went dry with lust. She appeared to note his helpless stare, but nonetheless, her eyes blazed twin flames of ire magnified through lenses that reflected the light of the fire. And suddenly, he could swear he could smell *her*...the familiar musky scent of a woman, of smoky seduction from long ago.

Suspicion ate at him, nagged until he had no choice but to demand, "Who are you?"

She smiled wickedly, baring perfect, sparkling white teeth. "I told you. I'm Jane."

Wary hesitation plagued him. He studied her further, noting all the differences. Of course she was Jane, he thought with a sigh. It had been a foolish thought to wonder if this woman could be Jewel Dublin, the woman who'd walked out on him years ago without a peep since. He swept her with an assessing gaze. No, his ex-lover couldn't possibly be one and the same with this person. But even though everything else appeared different, the personalities were strangely similar. Vince inhaled deeply, attempting to dispel the tension. The combination of anger, confusion and desire she'd stirred in him wouldn't settle. He was clearly losing his ever-loving mind! Fantasizing, wondering if one person—who obviously wasn't—could be another. Hell, did he miss her that much?

No, it couldn't be. Or maybe... No. He just wasn't sure how he felt about Jewel Dublin anymore.

But he was sure of one thing. This woman wasn't who she claimed to be, and she was definitely up to something. He couldn't quite put a finger on it, but it would come to him eventually. He'd get it out of her one way or another.

He scooped up his bowl and turned. Dropping it in the sink on top of the ice, he snarled, "Yeah, and I'm Tarzan. Now—"

They both turned as the door flew open and crashed against the wall. Wind and snow blew in, and suddenly, out in the tumult of the storm, it was as if someone had flipped a switch. The dull gray of a winter's day turned to pitch-black night. A white tornado of snow whirled, moaned and swept across the room until it reached the fire. Biting, chilly air filled the bungalow, and the warmth of their breath turned to puffs of white condensation.

With a loud buzzing noise, the twister spun and snuffed out the fire.

Still in his damp boxers and no shirt, he shivered in the darkness. And he knew this meant one thing. They would have to unite physically to survive, or freeze to death before this nightmare ended. For some reason, Jennie was deriving wicked pleasure out of throwing the two of them, different as night and day, together in this dream.

"Vince?" Her voice, husky and trembling in the dark, came to him warm and thick, as if the fire had been stoked.

He moved awkwardly through the room, feeling his way to the door. "Yes?"

"I-I'm scared..." Her teeth chattered. "A-and I'm freezing."

"Me too, Jane." He pushed against the strong winds until he had the door shut and latched. "But there's only one way to get warm. And you're not going to like it."

He turned and groped for her in the dark.

Chapter Four

Not going to like it? Jewel shivered with anticipation, knowing her life depended on him — and his on her. There was no way to escape this dilemma. She'd taken the only blanket off the bed. It was wrapped around her this very moment and she was still freezing. She could recall with sharp clarity that he wore nothing but boxers and a smooth suit of rippled, bare flesh. It would take no more than an hour in these sub-zero temperatures to turn them both to blocks of ice.

He fumbled for her hand. As biting cold whirled around them, he led her to the bed.

"Take off the blanket."

"But —"

"Don't argue with me, Jane. Do you want to die?"

"No, of course I don't, but —"

"Then take it," he growled, snatching the quilt from her, "*off!*"

"No, you can't…do that!"

She sucked in a quick breath when the cold air assaulted the flesh of her naked body. Immediately, she stooped and wrapped her arms around her torso. Her nipples drew up in painful protest. Goose bumps covered her body and she shivered uncontrollably. All she could think was she needed to be wrapped in warmth once again, to curl up and escape the harsh temperature of this nightmare.

Relief proved to come sooner than later. She heard a rustling sound followed by a squeak of the bedsprings. And all at once, she found herself sprawled over the wall of his chest. He adeptly positioned the cover across her backside, cocooning them both inside the quilt. The sudden rush of his breath on her cheek, the wild, manly scent of him, all played havoc on her raw nerves. Her blood thawed when it became apparent he'd stripped the wet boxers off. His soft penis came in contact with her juncture, and a jolt equivalent to a bolt of lightning struck her womb. His arms went around her, holding her tight against his quivering, muscular frame.

"No...please," she choked. Stiffening, Jewel warred with the pain and pleasure of being so close, so very intimate with him once again.

"Shh, I won't eat you alive." His palms moved up and down her back, dipped low to massage her ass. "I'm warming you. Warming me. Now relax and just enjoy the relief of it."

She knew his point couldn't be refuted. If only she had an out, if only she could devise some alternative. But total darkness and incomprehensible low temperatures were definitely disadvantages without solutions. Wet clothing, one blanket available within the walls of a strange cabin and being lost on some deserted island who-knew-where, didn't help matters either. Her only hope was that she might wake up eventually and find herself back in her narrow little convent bed.

Oh, but for now, she certainly occupied a different bed. With the man she still loved beyond reason, but couldn't have. Just thinking about that day so long ago when she'd come to him, finally getting up the nerve to ask where their relationship was going. And why not?

They'd been together as a couple for over a year and they'd practically been living together for months. They were happy and inseparable. And she'd had some news to break to him, life-altering news for them both.

But it hadn't gotten that far. He'd made it clear he was perfectly happy using her, taking things at his speed, taking his time deciding if he wanted to spend the rest of his life with her.

It was true that she'd let her temper get the better of her when she should have stayed and talked things out with him. And it was also true that she'd deliberately withheld that news from him out of fear, pride and a sort of retaliation for the pain that had ripped through her heart at his rejection. But there had been no excuse for his lack of pursuit of her after she'd walked out on him. He could have called, but he'd chosen to cut her completely from his life. He could have sought her out, but he'd preferred to spend his time taking up the lifestyle of a cocky playboy.

The car accident that night had only made things worse. Even as she lay in a weeklong coma, even while her battered body had undergone surgery and struggled to heal, and even when her heart had fought to beat, still he didn't come to her. Still, he'd rejected her, making it apparent—once she'd awakened to find he hadn't been at her bedside for a single minute—that she no longer mattered in his life. Her proposition to him to settle down, to form a plan of where their lives were headed, had been viciously crammed back down her throat. She'd needed to know those intentions *before* dropping the bomb on him, but it hadn't gotten that far.

And so here she was, back in bed with the man who hadn't cared enough to come after her, who hadn't cared enough to be at her comatose side as she'd teetered on the edge of death. This was a man who hadn't even bothered to inquire further as to the nature of her important news. This was a man who still to this day did not know what had motivated her to suddenly place more importance on his intentions where she was concerned.

But he would never know her secret. Never. The last thing she wanted was his pity, or his regret weighed down heavily with obligation. Oh, no, the last thing she'd allow was the sacrifice of her self-respect for a jerk like Vince Santiago.

"Mm, you smell good," he whispered in her ear, sending a sinful ripple of fire through her veins.

"Don't. Please, don't." She didn't move, for her limbs were filling with a delicious, languid heat she couldn't quite resist. Together, their bodies quickly warmed the bubble of space they huddled in. Gradually, the shivering subsided, replaced by relaxed limbs that thrived with his nearness. Despite the instinctual need to bolt from his arms, the temptation of comfort and warm bliss lured her.

He cupped the cheeks of her rear, pressing her pussy into his hardening cock. Her lips separated, and the pressure of his hands forced her legs to fall open on either side of his hips, while her clit abraded against the silky rod of him. She held in a gasp when she throbbed unwillingly against him, and a gush of liquid escaped her vagina.

She tried to close her thighs, but he lifted his knees, preventing her defensive move. "Vince, you mustn't—" and his mouth found hers in the darkness.

"Jane..." His large hands threaded in her hair, holding her head in place so that she was forced to keep her mouth against his. He sucked in her bottom lip and she groaned as sharp nips of pleasure-pain raced to her core. His tongue swept her lips, and he kissed the corners of her mouth. Mesmerized, she held still as he angled her head to draw first her top lip, then her bottom, into his mouth. "Damn, but I want you. Please, don't fight me anymore."

"This isn't right," she protested, but the weak tone of her own voice told them both she hadn't the willpower to withstand his charms. And she hated herself for being such a weakling.

"That's bullshit." He rolled her over and rose above her. She moaned against his mouth as he filled one hand with her breast. Cupping its fullness, he adeptly twisted and pulled the nipple between his thumb and index finger, just the way she remembered, just the way she'd fantasized about for the last four years. The sensation had her lifting her pelvis to press her juncture against the thigh he'd thrown across her hips. Her wetness dragged over his thigh, seeming to search on its own in the dark for his manhood.

As her mouth sampled the flavor of wine on his tongue, her cunt hungered for the drug of his cock. Warring with indecision, she knew she could have him if she chose to. But did she want to chance a broken heart again? Did she want to relinquish the power she held over him, even if he was oblivious to that unspoken control? She could have him and he'd never know it was Jewel Dublin.

But she would.

"You've wanted me, Jane, ever since you laid eyes on me," he accused, his hand darting down to find the hardness of her clit. "See? There's the proof."

She whimpered and arched her back as he expertly strummed her. Waves of ecstasy taunted her just out of reach.

He hurt you, Jewel, he hurt you, and doesn't even remember you. Fight him. Fight him with every ounce of your strength!

"No." She rolled her head from side to side, even as his finger increased speed.

You can't...allow this.

"Yes, babe, yes." And he rammed a pair of fingers inside her. She cried out, her eyelids fluttering against the assault as her hips rose to meet his thrust. Her head whirled out of orbit while her pussy fought the blazing streaks of shooting, wet stars.

"Vince...I can't—you can't. No!" She flipped to her side, turning her back to him. But he persevered, keeping his arm around her and his fingers inside her. Her back pressed against his chest and she felt every smooth plane, every swell of taut muscle. Against her ass, his long, thick cock pressed into her fleshy cheeks. With each plunging movement of his fingers, he rammed his rod against her rear, and she could imagine it sliding into her, taking her with devastating power. As his ragged breath teased her ear, she closed her eyes and concentrated on the rising sensations. The practiced movement of his hand bombarded her with the edges of orgasm, hovering just out of reach.

You must... Oh God, you must what? Oh yes, yes. Gotta have it, Jewel. So good, so delicious. He's here, he's with you. And he's making you feel so good!

"That's it, baby," he coaxed, his voice ragged, strained. He finger-fucked her with a frenzy, massaging her clit with his thumb simultaneously, expertly. "Yes. Let it go. Go with it, honey."

She cried out, her scream echoing within the four small walls. Her body stiffened as shards of tiny nebular explosions detonated in her pussy. Each one moved out, catching fire, combusting into larger flames that rippled out from the center of her universe, out along every nerve ending. She gasped in a breath that caught behind her breastbone, and saturated her lungs with the scent of his sweat and arousal. The taste buds in her mouth tingled and watered, as did her passage. Her muscles jolted with spasm after spasm of ecstasy.

"Oh...oh, God," she gulped.

"Wow." He withdrew his fingers and shifted to draw her under him, his fully hard penis brushing her inner thigh. The movement had the effect of ice-cold water over sleepy warmth.

Her eyelids flew open. "What—what are you doing?"

Though they remained in pitch-blackness, she could sense his expression, the snap of surprise in his dark eyes, the set of his jaw. "I'm going to slide into you, pleasure myself and you. Again. What else?"

She planted her hands on that mass of muscle and pecs and shoved. "No. No you're not." The ramifications of what she'd just allowed him to do slapped her square in the ego. Mortification, shame and unfathomable regret took hold with a mighty vengeance. Tears of self-hatred stung behind her eyes, threatening to spill.

"What? Wait a minute..." He took her chin in his hand, turning her face toward his in the dark. She caught the aroma of her traitorous juices on his fingers and jerked her face toward the wall.

You fool! You stupid, idiot fool. You're losing ground, losing the upper hand. This is the man who broke your heart. You can't *forget that!*

The memories, happy overshadowed by deep, deep pain were exhumed, and tears of anger rolled down her cheeks. The wetness chilled on her face, icicles of her sorrow for what could and should have been. But wasn't.

"Oh shit, are you crying?" He sighed and rolled away from her.

She refused to answer him, and instead, turned her back on him, gritting her teeth to force away the tears.

"Jane." He set a hand on her shoulder. She stiffened against the scalding heat of it. Automatically, as if burned, he jerked his hand back. "I'm — I'm sorry. Did I hurt you? I mean — "

Did you hurt me?

She couldn't stop it. The burst of sobs mixed with hysterical laughter wrenched from somewhere deep in her soul. Curling into a ball, she prayed to Luke.

Luke, please. Please wake me up. This nightmare has got to end before I lose my mind. Why are you doing this to me?

"Oh hell, Jane." Vince shifted, rising up on an elbow, his hand stroking her arm. "What's wrong, babe?"

"Don't!" She slapped his hand away. "Don't touch me anymore. Do you hear me? And don't call me babe!"

A long, quiet pause ensued. Grumbling, he turned so that the length of his back pressed into hers. The small double-sized bed clearly would not allow her any free space. Forced to feel his warmth, to share the blanket with the creep, she doused at the tears and sniffled.

It was long after Vince's even breathing told her he slumbered on in contentment, that sleep finally overtook her. Plagued by dreams of searing hands and potent kisses, she slept with the man she hated. And loved.

* * * * *

Vince's catnap proved to be far from contented. Everywhere he turned, Jewel taunted him in dreams. He drifted back, receding into a sleep-induced memory that had been buried for over four years.

He saw her with crystal clarity in his sleepy mind, the seductive emerald of her eyes as he entered her for the first time. They widened and then went limpid with the first innocent throes of near-orgasmic passion and surprise. She'd sure fooled him by the way she'd come alive in his arms like a wanton, practiced siren. He hadn't known she was a virgin until that profound moment, too late to take back her broken barrier. He tossed in bed, remembering the thrill of it as he slumbered, imagining her tightness gloving his cock as it had that first night.

"Ah..." she winced and moaned simultaneously in his dream of remembered reality. Vince slipped deeper into her, deeper into that dream. He could smell her sweet, earthy scent, could almost taste her juices in his mouth. Her warm, soft body lay below him, her legs spread wide in innocent welcome. Animal need to ravish, to drive himself forcefully into her, overtook his soul. But he fought it. Tenderness tamed the beastly instinct. Jewel whimpered below him, sobbing for more, begging to be taken to that never-before-seen place that drifted just out of her reach.

Jesus, but the battle to get inside her shocked him, snug and sticky-wet. With urgency, he pushed further and met with tighter resistance. The *pop* sensation, followed by her gasp made him pause. He remembered the stunned thought... Had he just christened a virgin? He looked down into her eyes, narrowed now in passion-edged pain, and watched as the pupils dilated and the lids fluttered over two crazed nuggets of green. And an unknown affection washed over him like the tide in a hurricane.

"You're...you're..." He swallowed, struggling to maintain control while his balls tightened, ached to explode. "A virgin?"

"Was," she whispered huskily, even as she started to rock her hips against him instinctively. Moist tightness stroked him; her alluring perfume filled his nostrils.

And he lost it, utterly lost control...

"Vince. *Vince!*"

At first, it had been Jewel's voice calling to him within the orgasmic, blissful dream. But gradually, it turned to Jane's husky, panicked tone.

"Vince. Oh God, Vince, *please* wake up!"

Jewel slipped from his arms and faded into nothingness. His eyes flew open. He stared at the beamed ceiling struggling to catch his breath. Loss and empty pain squeezed his heart fresh and raw. The fire blazed in the hearth once again, he could tell that by the dancing light upon the ceiling above him. The room no longer felt like a walk-in freezer, evidenced by the fact that the blanket was gone and the heat of the fire tucked pleasantly around his limbs.

And his cock throbbed with heavy desire. He'd awakened with a painful, hot hard-on.

He turned his head, glancing at Jane. She lay on her back, her face turned toward him. Her body appeared stiff and unyielding, her hands were down at her sides. He slid his gaze over her ripe, naked body and groaned. Instinctively, he started to lift a hand to cup one breast, to feed the need the dream had infected him with.

But he couldn't move. Attempting to struggle against the strange force, he lay paralyzed, his entire body motionless. With the exception of being able to turn his head, he realized every ounce of his strength had been drained from him. An invisible shield appeared to be holding him in place, restraining him against rising from the bed. Yet every cell of his skin and bones thrived and tingled with anticipation of the unknown.

"Vince..." Jane's brow furrowed, her eyes shimmered with fear. "I can't move a muscle. Help me. Please help me."

"Sweetheart, if I could, I would." He raised his head and nearly choked as the edge of the invisible panel jabbed his throat. "But I can't move either."

"Lord, help me," Jane breathed, her eyes shutting in denial. "This can't be happening. This *isn't* happening."

"Oh, but it is."

The familiar voice had Vince jerking his head around in search of his old college friend. "Luke Slayton? Is that you?"

"Luke!" Jane sighed, her gaze searching for the source of the voice. "Oh, thank God you've come back. I'm stuck—we're stuck. You've got to help us."

"Hello, *Jane* and Vince. What's up, buddy?"

"Well..." He chuckled, glancing down at his stiff cock. "The usual. But the more important topic than chitchat here is, we need help. Not counting the fact that Jane and I've been somehow glued in place, we're stuck here on this weird island. Can you help us?" He paused, darted his gaze about. "Hey, where the hell are you?"

Luke suddenly appeared with the tune of a jingle, levitating above Jane. Lying sprawled on his side, his head propped on a fist, he posed in complete, relaxed nakedness. His buff body gleamed in the firelight, every muscle outlined by shadows entwined in soft light. Vince noted with dismay that Luke's dick stood fully erect against his flat abdomen, almost pulsing with need. He'd seen his pal in the raw many times before, including during the threesomes with an occasional woman they'd shared, but this was ridiculous and completely out of context.

"Jesus, Luke, get some goddamn clothes on."

"Oh, God..." Jane gulped, her eyes wide as she had no choice but to stare up at the nude man draped above her. Her gaze moved helplessly to his cock.

"But I quite adore him naked." That from Jennie, her sultry voice laced with mischief.

"Jennie. So, the genie returns. Go ahead, show yourself."

Vince heard a snap of fingers and she appeared above him, hovering in the same position as Luke, though propped on the opposite side facing him. And in the buff as all gorgeous get-out. He couldn't help but sweep his gaze over her. Hell, he had no other choice. She floated mere inches above him. Her seductive, tropical-laced scent filled his lungs, tantalizing, playing havoc on his already throbbing tool. To have Jane at his side, knowing she saw the same stimulating sights he did, and an attractive, nude couple all just out of reach, was pure torture.

And plain mean.

"What the *hell* is going on here?"

"My husband and I were just about to make love. We thought," Jennie purred, reaching over to stroke Luke's rod, eliciting an instant groan from him, "that we'd share it with you two stubborn islanders."

"Vince? You know Luke?" Jane croaked.

"Oh, yeah. I know the bastard all right." He couldn't take his eyes from Jennie's expert talent, and he longed to have Jane's hand around him in much the same manner.

"But he's a genie. Where did you ever meet a genie?" Jane asked, wide-eyed.

"Genie? Like Jennie?"

"That's right, pal," Luke said on a groan, his eyelids fluttering as Jennie reached down, wetted her hand with her own juices, then resumed her expert hand caressing. "A lot has changed since I last saw you years ago. I've died and gone to Xanthian heaven, gotten married. And I'm enjoying—ah! My eternal life immensely."

"So this is your doing, all of this?"

Luke chuckled deep and wicked from the depths of his soul. His voice echoed softly in the fire-lit room. The mixed scent of smoke and sexual arousal filled the cottage. "No, not all of it. My Jennie, here, she's got an important job to do, and I'm happily assisting her. But I did suggest you as her very first mission to repair."

"Repair? What the fuck do you mean by that?"

Luke reached over and cupped one of Jennie's breasts. The dark nipple sprang to life. Her full cherry lips pursed and forced out a whimper. Vince itched to reach up and sample the other globe, but his body remained immobile.

"Just like my lover told you when you released her from the bottle. It's a sorry life you've got there. Time to do something about it. So here you are."

"With a strange woman on a strange island—with weird fucking goings-on?" He ignored the grind of Jane's teeth, the sudden huffs of breath that escaped her nostrils. "You've lost your damn mind, Luke Slayton. Must have had a shortage of oxygen when you died, there, pal. And I hardly see how my life is any of your freaking business."

Luke's eyes narrowed and aqua flames ignited there. "Though you're standing—um, *laying*, rather—on shaky ground, asshole, you're my best friend. You've had a…situation going on right under your cocky nose for many years. Now if you'd just open your eyes, trust your instincts, quit ignoring them and take a good look, you might understand. I want you to be happy again. Because I care about your life, man. That's all."

"And what about me?" Jane demanded, her face set concrete-permanent with anger. "I don't know any of you. Why me? Why did you abduct me and force me to endure…him?"

Jennie winked at Jane, her eyes glittering gold nuggets in the firelight. "You already know the answer to that, *Jane*. Now if you'd just open your heart and dispense with the martyrdom, you just might get some long-awaited answers."

Jane gasped. "Martyrdom? You bitch. How dare you accuse me of such a thing?" She struggled against the force that held her in place, and Vince could see in her eyes that if Jane were free, Jennie just might be a dead genie by now.

Jennie threw her head back and giggled, her long raven hair falling down to tickle Vince's cheek. He wiggled his nose and blew the silky lock away.

"Jane, honey, if it weren't for the fact you've been banished into your own bottle of pain for over four years, I'd show you just how much of a bitch I can be. But," she said with a smile vaguely rimmed with sarcasm, "I'm a good genie, here to attain a wondrous goal. And that does not include punishing you at the moment."

A tear of frustrated ire pooled in the corner of Jane's eye. "Then release me. This is cruel, and definitely a punishment I don't deserve."

"Oh, that's debatable. I will say, however, that *this* will be your punishment." She sat up and reached for Luke's erection. "But believe me, it won't hurt you in the least." And she ducked her head, swallowing up her husband's cock.

Luke tossed back his head and moaned, "Yes! Oh Jennie, I thought we'd never get back to this. Ah, yes, baby. *Yes!*"

She ringed him with her hand, opening her mouth wide and bobbing up and down on his stiffness. Her other hand cupped his balls, massaging expertly so that he grunted his approval. Vince's hands struggled to fist beneath the paralyzing blanket. He longed to stab his hands into Jane's hair just the way Luke did Jennie's, guiding her blowjob. The two floated above him and Jane, their bodies spinning together this way and that. The movement left nothing to the imagination. They were forced to observe the lovemaking from every arousing angle. Scents and lusty aromas wafted beneath Vince's nose, making his blood pound as it coursed through his veins. His cock filled with a desperate need to plunge into wet, tight softness.

He heard a soft whimper from Jane and turned to see her mouth in an O. She kept shutting her eyes in defiance then opening them, obviously unable to resist the show. Panting in obvious arousal, her curiosity forced her to observe the two bodies above them. Just watching her watch them turned him on to such a degree, he vowed at that moment that he would have her before this dream was over. And if the genies released him after this mandatory voyeurism session, he would have her now. That he knew with every ounce of his being. He glanced down and studied the voluptuous curves of her body. Dark areolas stood tight and proud, peaked upon her breasts. Her legs were held in place, spread, ready for his entry, and he could swear he saw pearl-like beads of her juices glistening on the dark blonde curls of her mons. He licked his lips, imagining lapping up that nectar, almost tasting the sweet, salty flavor in his mouth already.

His eyes drifted back to the sexy performance. The firelight played on every nuance of their bodies, bathing them in a passionate glow as Luke yanked Jennie's head up and devoured her mouth. Stabbing his hand into her hair, he spun her around so that he sat up with her cunt in his face. Vince could smell the musky scent of her, and the torture of watching his best friend dine on fresh, eager pussy nearly pushed him over the edge. Hands and mouths were everywhere, on breasts plucking at nipples, skimming asses, fingering assholes, cupping balls and stroking hard and soft flesh. The two sex-crazed genies couldn't get enough of each other, and their very vocal, robust intent became apparent. To be turned on and to turn on, to bring forth a sexual craze in their spectators that could not be denied — and to slake their own lust.

"Ah, Jesus, Luke." He raised his head, tried to escape the invisible blanket that pinned them to the bed. "You're a cruel bastard."

Luke merely chuckled deep, his voice muffled by silky folds and Jennie's very strident cries of passion. The three-dimensional form of their bodies spun then, so that he could see up-close-and-personal the sudden penetration of Jennie's slit with Luke's enormous cock.

Vince groaned in unison with them, delighted when the sweet song of Jane's reluctant moan carried to his ears. He sympathized completely with her torment. But he couldn't take his eyes off the fucking motions as the genie's crotches loomed close, spraying out the mouth-watering scent of sex. He was sure even Jane could smell it. There was no way she could miss every glistening bump, bulge and hole as Jennie got fucked by her husband before their very captive eyes. With the exception of touch, each of Vince's senses were heightened and bombarded by the blatant acts before him. The knowledge that Jane had to be feeling the same depth of arousal he felt only intensified his suffering.

Just when he thought he could take the agony no more, just when he swore he'd come without a single bit of physical stimulation, Jennie screamed her release.

"Oh, stars!" she moaned, clutching Luke to her naked breast.

Astonished, Vince stared agog as her eyes turned a flaming ruby-red. "Yes! Oh, gods, *yes!*" she cried.

Luke grunted, his large hands clutching Jennie's ass cheeks so far open, Vince could see her tight little asshole spasm with her endless orgasm. Luke buried his face in her neck and groaned, "Finally. Ah, my Jennie in a bottle..." Still hungry, he claimed one nipple and drew it into his mouth.

The movement pushed her over that final edge. They shattered into tiny, multi-colored diamonds. Their unison cry of bliss sang out in melody with a tinkling tune. Gradually, the shards of Jennie and Luke disappeared and faded into the ceiling.

* * * * *

Jewel stared blankly at the beams and slats of the ceiling. The only sounds were those of the crackling fire and Vince's heavy pants. Knowing him — and feeling the damp mess that pooled between her thighs — he had to have gotten royally turned on by that show, also. But she refused to look at him for fear her pride would crumble and she'd beg him to ease her discomfort. Despite the meddling genies' intent, Jewel would hold to her scruples. Martyrdom! Oh, the nerve of that haughty bitch! Okay, so they'd managed to get her all in a frustrated, sexual tizzy, but she'd prove she could outwit them. Even though the genies had the obvious, unfair advantage of keeping them both immobile and naked at each other's sides.

As if the thought of it had released him, Vince sat up. "I'm free!"

She darted a look at the lean length of his back, the broad shoulders. Her pulse fluttered, but she ignored it easily. "Good. And next will be me." Jewel started to rise. Meeting with resistance, she dropped her head back to the pillow. "Oh, God, no. Please don't do this to me. *Please*."

Vince flexed his arms and legs. Leaning back, he stuffed a pillow under his armpit. On his side, he stared down at her. The rabid gleam in his eyes, and the huge erection that brushed her hand, told her everything she needed to know. He wasn't going to let his prey loose from the genies' trap, even if he had the power to do so.

"I don't think God has anything to do with this," he rasped, dragging a fingertip from her shoulder to her wrist. Shivers of reluctant anticipation racked her body, but still, the invisible shield held her in place so that even the involuntary movement was suppressed.

"Don't touch me, Vince. I mean it."

"And what are you going to do about it if I do?" He shifted his hand to her knee and massaged it. Languid pleasure pooled there, and hot blood moved in a slow ripple of waves up her thigh, right toward the target.

She swallowed a lump of regret. "I don't want your hands on me, and I have a right to demand that you keep them to yourself." She only darted her eyes and refused to turn her head toward him, to give in to him even that small bit. The sensation of being held down, unable to move, unable to close her spread legs, played havoc with her mind. On the one hand, frustration seethed within her and she longed to cover herself from his smoldering gaze. Even without looking, she could feel his burning eyes touching on every cell of her body. But on the other hand, some wicked little corner of her mind screamed for him to touch her, to bring her to that pinnacle that only Vince Santiago could.

Which was ridiculous because he'd made it very clear all those years ago that he had no intention or desire to keep her in his life. He'd been using her, as he would now if she permitted it.

But she wasn't going to allow it, no matter how strong his male magic was, and no matter what sort of spells those damn genies conjured up. She'd fight them all. She'd prevail.

"Stop it right now!"

With his head propped on a fist, he looked down watching the trail of his own hand. That scalding-hot palm moved up her thigh in slow agony. It bypassed her pussy, but he darted one finger out as the hand went upward over her hip. Barely brushing her right labia lip, the shock of it brought forth an involuntary cry. Her passage spasmed, oozing out more juices from her vagina.

"See? You want it. You know you do. Your heart races, your blood begins to boil, your pulse pounds hard and hot, deep inside your belly."

"That's...that's a lie." And she sucked in a breath when the calloused fingers slid up her rib cage and cupped her breast.

"No...stop..."

He rolled the already hard nipple between his fingers. An electric bolt shot through her blood, settling low in her womb. He ducked his head and the familiar scent of his shampoo entwined with light sweat filled her nostrils. The aroma intensified when she looked down at him as he neared her breast, her nose becoming buried in his thick head of dark hair. Unable to resist, Jewel inhaled, her eyes fluttering closed as the smells tipped off random memories of a love now lost. Showering together, running her fingers through that hair as he caressed her neck with his talented mouth, frolicking in bed on a Sunday morning as he wrestled her to the mattress, ending in inevitable, mind-blowing penetration.

But the thoughts scattered when his warm mouth closed over her nipple. She cried out, fighting to release her arms. Her first instinct had been to push him away. But now, now that he swirled his tongue around the areola, combusting her core into an inferno, she longed to wrap her arms around his head, to cradle him there so he couldn't cease the delicious, expert, wet dance of his tongue.

"Ah, Jane..." He came over her, settling between her spread legs. The pressure of his lower abdomen against her mons soothed like the relieved scratch of an intense itch. But she soon realized it only initiated a new itch, and the frustration of not being able to "scratch" became a bittersweet torture. The heat from his body melded with the pressure of his hands on her breasts, kneading, cupping, massaging. Her traitorous nipples tightened into knots that begged for his mouth, his touch. He obliged and Jewel longed to wrap herself around him. If only she could be freed...

He worked his way up her chest to her neck, sending little shivers of desire through her. Nipping and sucking the flesh there, he barely touched the tip of his cock to her vee. The contact tempted her cruelly beyond reason. Oh, how she longed to buck upward, to force him to sink it inside her! Determined to have him, she struggled to move, to meet his demands. But the force continued to hold her immobile and at Vince's mercy.

Suddenly, his mouth covered hers. She tasted wine and the sweet flavor of Vince, drinking in the warm wetness of him. His tongue swept her mouth and he moaned against her lips, deepening the kiss. Jewel took and took, starved for him after so long denied. Her hard nipples pressed into his own, reveling in the sturdy wall of his chest against her soft one.

"Perfect, so perfect," he whispered as he broke free of her mouth to start yet another trail of madness. He kissed her jaw, then the crook of her neck. The warm wetness fanned the flames, her pussy gushed with sticky sap. His wide hands caressed her shoulders, and he followed that with nips and licks at her collarbones. Down he went over breast and peak, down into valleys and planes. He gripped her rib cage on either side and dragged his mouth back and forth across her belly.

She panted, crying out when he dipped his tongue into her navel. "Vince...I...I—oh no, oh, you can't do that—*oh*!"

Thrashing her head from side to side, it was her only defense against the feel of his tongue swiping her labia, her clit, her slit. Due to the shield, he couldn't lift her body up to eat her at a better angle, but there was no need. His expertise proved to be creative. On all fours, he turned so that his knees straddled her head. Above her, his stiff cock poised proud, the long, veiny length of it so familiar and tempting. His sac was drawn up tight, just as it used to be when he would become wildly excited and close to release. Oh, heavens, it had been so long since she'd been this up-close and personal with him! Inhaling, she caught the aroma of animalistic arousal and sea-salty skin. Licking her lips, she longed to take him into her mouth.

"Vince...?"

"What, baby?" he breathed, ducking to press a kiss to first her inner right thigh, then the left. His breath fanned her skin, and she thought there could be nothing more beautiful and cruel at the same time, than to be held captive here in this predicament at this very moment.

"I...I want it."

"Tell me what you want, Jane." He swirled his tongue around her clit, still holding his cock away from her face. One finger slid slowly into her.

She screamed, her voice echoing against the walls of the cottage. He'd branded her, and she thought the orgasm was about to wash through her in that one swipe of the tongue, that one slide of the finger. But it didn't. The torture continued.

"Your dick," she panted. "I want your dick in my mouth." God, she sounded pathetic, and it irked her on a level somewhere way back behind all the pleasure. But greed won out and she ignored it.

"And I definitely want your pussy."

With that, he buried his face between her sticky legs and guided his cock into her mouth, all in one smooth movement. The familiar salty flavor and silk-over-steel feel against her tongue made her audibly sigh with joy. She equated it to being on a diet for four years, then finally sinking your teeth into that sweet piece of moist chocolate cake. Relief, heaven, forbidden bliss.

Still being held in place, unable to move a muscle, Jewel took the assault in grateful stride. As her tongue swirled around the large, round head, lapping up the zesty taste of him, he alternated swiping her clit and fucking her hole with his long tongue. She no longer had to fantasize about it, to remember the vivid sensations of his expert lovemaking. It was here, now, all over her, in her.

Fires blazed in places she didn't know existed inside her. Her hands tried to ball into fists. She longed to draw her knees up and tip her pelvis up so he could get deeper, closer to her g-spot that throbbed with the promise of coming relief. As if in answer to her needs, he concentrated on flickering his tongue over her clit, while something sank into her canal, something thick and long and flesh-like. The wet, satiny feel of his tongue, coupled with the fullness inside her, now showed extreme promise of fulfillment. She sucked hard on him, taking him deep into her throat, even as he rammed the object in and out of her. Jewel heard the song of his moans and felt the vibration of them on her nub.

She paused and drew in a breath around his dick when the boundary of the orgasm neared. He yanked his cock from her mouth and perched himself above her as before.

"No! Wait. What are you...? Oh, shit. Oh...oh *shit*!" She felt his arms shift and heard the buzzing tune right before the object began to vibrate with blessed accuracy, right smack-dab on her g-spot. Able only to lift her head, she peered down the length of her body to see him pumping a fleshy vibrator in and out of her cunt.

"Where..." She couldn't talk, couldn't breathe. "Where did you get that?"

"Mm," he mumbled as he sucked her clit in between his teeth. She jolted against the fire, struggling to hear his words. "Don't know. Just appeared. The genies, you know."

Ah, the genies. But she didn't have time to ponder it, to either thank or blast them for this bizarre event in her life. Her head bobbed while her body remained still. As the white-hot slivers of release shattered around her, she groaned and slowly shut her eyes, soaking in the myriad of sensations as the vibrator slid into her wetness and Vince's tongue wiggled over her clit.

Her heart thudded painfully in her chest. Sweat dribbled down her neck. The sweltering room came back into focus. "Oh. My. Gosh."

Vince chuckled and tossed aside the vibrator. He turned back around to settle between her thighs once again. "I second that," he said, his voice strained. She watched as his eyes darkened to the shade of sin. And knew his intent at that instant, for she suddenly realized she'd come, but he hadn't yet.

He kissed her on the mouth and she tasted herself there. Something about it stirred up the beginnings of desire once again. But she couldn't go on this way, further endearing her heart to a man who hadn't wanted her. It would just end in the same painful conclusion. And she couldn't take that kind of hurt anymore.

"Jane...you're so hot, so irresistible."

God, how she wished he'd quit calling her that. And she wished she could get loose. Looking around, she called out, "Let me out of here, damn it, Luke. You both got what you wanted. Now. Let. Me. Go." With each word, she struggled against the force, but to no avail.

"I think what they want," Vince said, gathering her breasts up in his hands, "is for us *both* to come, and for us to consummate this coming together correctly."

He rammed his cock into her wetness before she had time to assimilate the pleasant feel of her breasts in his warm palms. Pussy already tingling again with the meaning of his words, followed by his aggressive actions, she groaned aloud. "Oh! Oh, Vinnie..."

Her breath caught in her throat. Vince stilled his movements, allowing them both to become accustomed to his entry. Tears sprang to her eyes behind the lenses of her glasses she refused to remove in order to keep up her façade. To be filled by him again after so long had a profound, painful effect on her heart. *Okay, just this once, Jewel. It's too late to stop it anyway. Partake of it just this one time, savor it, but don't allow it again. You can't risk that kind of loneliness and despair anymore. You just can't.*

Resolved to be strong and firm from here on out, she decided to take full advantage while she had him here between her legs once again.

Luke, please, please release me.

For what reason, Jewel Dublin?

A tear rolled down her cheek even as Vince took her mouth tenderly with his. The manner in which he kissed her tore at her emotions and had her breath stilling in her lungs. She could feel the warmth of his body over hers, sense the weight of his hips, the fullness of her core as he filled it. The musky scent of him cocooned her, and his sweet flavor laced by her own syrup burst in her mouth. She longed to hold him to her just this once, to allow herself this one indulgence of imagining that his possession of her transcended her pain, that he loved her.

So I can wrap myself around him. Hold him close. So I can love him.

And with that thought, she heard a faint *pop*. She sighed when her arms relaxed and were able to rise up and wrap around his neck. Gathering him close as he buried himself to the hilt, she tested her legs, pleased when she discovered she could lock her ankles behind him. She tilted her pelvis so that he could reach that spot deep inside her that only he knew intimately. He groaned and dragged her up so that he kneeled in the bed. Jewel clutched him, throwing her head back as he devoured her breasts. The fire in the hearth blazed higher when he suckled at her nipple and gripped the cheeks of her ass, bouncing her up and down on his shaft. Even though he'd sunk himself into her depths, an urge welled up in her to be further impaled. The fullness of him inside her, the taste of his kiss as he moved from her breast to her mouth, the flicker of firelight on glistening flesh, all served to put her heart at risk once again.

But for now, there was one goal. And when he dipped his fingertip in her tight asshole and moaned out his release, she reached that objective with swift precision. Hot cum scalded her core, and her canal walls shuddered around the length of him, milking every drop from his balls. As the song of their simultaneous release died out, he tumbled with her to the mattress, still joined as one.

Jewel took one last moment to catch her breath and savor the feel of being in his arms before she pushed him away. His cock slipped from her, leaving him with the shocked look of rejection in those gorgeous eyes of his. There was an emptiness in her soul that she knew would never be filled by him ever again.

With a heavy, painful weight in her chest, she rolled away from him, cursing herself for opening that damn bottle.

* * * * *

Vince couldn't shake the shock, even now, thirty minutes later. With her back to him, he watched the rise and fall of her body as she breathed. Her long limbs rested limply as she slept on without a care. His gaze moved back to that spot again, down over the voluptuous curve of her hip…to her ass.

There was no mistaking this was Jewel Dublin. The initial proof had been when she'd called him "Vinnie" right after he'd buried his cock inside her. She was the only woman ever or since, to call him by his nickname. He'd definitely heard Jewel's voice calling out to him through the raspiness of Jane's. Instant awareness had nearly caused him to rip himself out of that suddenly familiar, tight tunnel. But wonder and joy at having her back in his arms had overtaken him.

Confession time, Vince. You missed her so bad, you wouldn't even admit it to yourself until now, until you finally had her back in your arms.

No, he hadn't been able to deny himself the woman who'd haunted his dreams for four years. And now, further proof that Jane was one and the same as Jewel, stared back at him from the warm, cushy flesh he'd just held in his hands during that phenomenal round of lovemaking. No other woman but Jewel Dublin had a tattoo of his name—first *and* last—on her ass, at least that he was aware of. The more he'd thought about her deceit as he lay here staring at that telling mark, the more the rage had set in. He squelched the urge to shake and awaken her and to demand to know what this was all about. But instead, he stretched out next to her, calm, calculating his next move, trying to examine her without waking her.

The soft strands of her sexy, faintly layered blonde hairstyle—previously long and black if his memory served him correctly—had fallen away from her neck. That had presented another piece of irrefutable evidence. The oblong, dark brown mole he'd always loved to kiss was there, right below the hairline at the nape of her neck. The ear that the movement of hair exposed revealed the six tiny holes in a line down the edge of the cartilage, though obviously and curiously, she'd allowed those much-adored holes to grow shut. He blinked and quietly rose on an elbow to study it closer. What was that? There, at the hairline above her ear, and along the ear itself... Scars. When had those scars gotten there, and what had caused them? Puzzled, he reached out to touch them, but jerked his hand back when she jolted in her sleep.

Something...*something* wasn't adding up here, but he couldn't quit put his finger on it. The nagging sense he'd had when he'd first met "Jane" now veered onto a whole new route. He now knew who she was, but something else troubled him. *Why* she was such a different-looking Jewel than he used to know. And why she'd chosen to deceive him.

He gently tugged the quilt up to her hips, but stopped when she stirred in her sleep. Halting the need to move up closer behind her, he fought the urge to tuck her into the crook of his body. The touch of the blanket against her skin brought a contented sigh from her, and she rolled over onto her back, one arm flung above her head. Free to examine her naked torso, he noted she'd obviously gone on a diet. Though he'd loved the plumpness of her former body, she now had a healthier shape. Not at all bone-thin like the models he'd bedded lately, but voluptuous, wholesome and well-nourished, without carrying the health risks of obesity. Ah, yes, the heavy frame had transformed into a curvy, solid and oh-so luscious package. Her abdomen wasn't flat and tight, but supple and soft. The waist wasn't tiny either, like the ones he'd grown accustomed to since she'd walked out on him. But it was small in comparison to her flared hips, accentuating the very womanly, hourglass figure. And those breasts! Much smaller than they'd been before, they were still an overabundance for even his large hands. His cock throbbed, remembering the feel of them against tongue and palm.

Vince sighed. *Oh, no. Down boy. Can't let that override the sudden priority here. Take it if you can get it, yes, but this whole dream, or whatever the hell it is, has become much more complex than you even imagined. Priorities, Vince. Just remember the main goal here.*

He went on to study her sleeping form. From his angle, her face was outlined by the firelight illuminating the room. Dark brown lashes fanned high cheekbones. His gaze followed the profile of the nose, small but marred with a slight lump that hadn't been there before. Even now, and even during their lovemaking session, she'd worn the spectacles. Mental images of her previous face filled his mind. He shut his eyes and struggled to compare this woman who now wore glasses, to the woman who'd never once worn them in all the time he'd known her. The vivid, green twin orbs blinked behind his lids. He saw them in his mind's eye, and suddenly he remembered...she'd always worn contacts. The sparkly look of her eyes, the almost unreal shade of green, the sometimes-bloodshot whites and excessive blinking at times. She'd worn them almost obsessively, so much so that he'd totally forgotten she'd had a sight deficit.

Vince combed a hand through his hair in disbelief and self-disgust. *What an idiot you were, Vince! There she'd been, right before your eyes, right beneath the palm of your hand, even in your arms, and you didn't see the real her,* this *woman.* Her hair had been dyed to black, her eyes disguised with brighter colored contacts and her body burdened with a good excess forty to fifty pounds. But wait a minute, he thought, placating his ignorance. She didn't wear a drop of makeup anymore, but back then, she'd worn it like a mask. That alone could fool any man, right? And her voice. Hell, all that coughing and choking she'd done when she'd arrived here. Must have made it gruffer, more difficult to hear the usual honey voice beneath the deep hoarseness.

He folded his arms behind his head and studied the beams in the ceiling. So many things about her were different, and so many still the same. Grinning, he thought of her temper and quick wit. Then there were the volatile, swift-changing emotions, the tender, easily bruised ego. And the fiery, passionate lover she could be. Yes, he thought, flicking a glance over at her scrumptious body. Some things hadn't changed.

But the real Jewel Dublin lay next to him. Like a butterfly, she'd shed her cocoon and bloomed. Inside and out, she'd stayed the same, yet grown into a stronger, more beautiful woman, adding layers and depth to her base.

And he supposed, he thought with regret, that it could be attributed to shedding Vince Santiago from her life as much as to the changes in hair and weight and contact lenses, and whatever else had been included in her unbelievable makeover.

But knowing her, he'd never be able to confront her and demand to know why she carried on this farce. He'd lose her all over again. Steel walls would go up in a second. Wise to her now, he knew his best trump card would be to play dumb until she slipped up or let the cat out of the bag with her temper. He chuckled to himself. Which would be the most likely scenario.

Damn, it was getting hot in here. Vince sat up slowly, so as not to awaken her, and slung his legs over the side of the bed. Rising, he crossed to the door and swung it open.

Darkness met his eyes. Blinking, he stepped out onto the small porch and waited for his vision to adjust.

He glanced around, looked down at his bare feet.

"Where the hell's the snow? And the freezing cold?" He leaped from the stoop and stood in the clearing. Sultry night air just tinged with an ocean breeze rustled around his naked body. A night owl hooted deep in the forest. Off in the distance, back through the thick forest and mangroves, he could hear the faint rush and pull of the tide as it crashed against the shore. The click-click of saw palmetto fronds fluttering against one another precluded the sudden gust of the scent of oranges mixed with sea.

"I'll be goddamned." Vince sighed, wondering what could be next from that asshole friend of his.

"Vince?"

He spun at the sound of her voice, now slightly less hoarse than it had been. But apparently, she hadn't noticed her cover was blown. She continued to speak.

"I...what's going on here?" He watched as she moved down the steps toward him, the blanket wrapped under her arms and tied in a knot at her cleavage. "The snow, it's gone. And I'm about to bake."

"No kidding. And it might help if you took off the thick quilt."

"Don't start with me." She lifted her chin, and by the intermittent moonbeams that sliced through the overhead trees, he could see the gleam of her anger magnified through the lenses of her glasses. "Just because I slept with you doesn't mean—"

Something caught his eye behind her. A flash, a flicker. "Oh hell..."

"Oh hell, what?" She paused, but went on when he merely stared at the space beyond her. "What? Vince, what the hell are you looking at?"

"Nothing. Absolutely nothing."

"You're making no sense." Jewel whirled around, promptly gasping. "Oh no. Oh God, please, no."

They stood together in the moonlit jungle and stared at the spot where the cottage had been. Like Jennie and Luke, it had vanished into thin air, leaving the two behind without shelter.

He jammed his hands on his hips and looked up into the cloud-puffed, tropical night sky. "Goddamn it, Luke. *Now* what?"

Chapter Five

Jewel gawked, removing her glasses in order to rub her eyes. Squinting, she knew there was no mistake. The bungalow where they'd taken shelter from the snowstorm, where she'd allowed Vince to make love to her just one more time, no longer existed.

"What are we going to do?" She hated the desperate note in her voice, but there was no stopping the panic that rose up and caged her in. "Where will we go? What if it rains or *snows* again, or there's a tornado or a hurri—"

"Jane."

"Hurricane?" she continued. "We could drown or…or die."

She rushed toward the spot where the cabin had been.

"Jane. No, wait. Don't—"

Maybe, just maybe it was there, but she just needed to get closer in order to see it.

"Jane! Goddamn it, I said…"

She tripped over something in the darkness. The *humph* of the wind whooshing from her lungs came out with a grunt.

"Don't," he finished with a sigh.

Pain sliced through her ankle across the very spot she'd scraped before. Only this time, excruciating fire shot through her leg. As if that weren't enough, she heard the sickening crack of plastic. Her glasses. God no, please don't let it be her glasses. He may recognize her without them, which would start a whole new round of tension-filled conflict. Sprawled on the sandy earth, she groped in the moon-dappled shadows. Her hand brushed something, then another object.

"Oh no. Oh no..." she groaned.

He was at her side before she could rise. His warm hand, no longer steady as it had been upon her flesh during lovemaking, now trembled as he gripped her upper arm.

"Are you okay?" He combed his hand through her hair, skimmed it over her body checking for injuries. She ignored the tender gesture, disregarded the fuzzy, breathtaking goo that wrapped about her heart. Her hair stood on end and she suppressed the instinct to sigh and nuzzle into his hand.

Remember, Jewel, you're someone else to him. His concern is not for you but for "another" woman whom he had no problem bedding. The cheating rat!

She shrugged away his hand and pulled herself to a sitting position on the forest floor. "Oh, fine and dandy. I scraped my ankle"—she touched the gash and hissed at the throbbing pain of it—"and broke my glasses in two." She glared up into the night sky. Insects and tree frogs buzzed and chirped around her. Fruity scents glazed by salty wind currents drifted in on a balmy night breeze. "Thank you *so* much, Luke." She couldn't hide the sarcasm in her husky voice. "And Jennie, too. This lovely little tropical vacation getaway is just what I needed."

Jewel huffed out a breath of disgust and hauled herself up, slapping Vince's hands away. She set her foot down and winced at the shooting pain in her ankle.

Clutching the two broken halves of her glasses, she wound up to toss them into the undergrowth. She cried out when Vince's hand closed around her wrist just before she winged the lenses.

"Don't be a fool. You lose those glasses, we could possibly die."

His eyes gleamed two black fires by the lunar light. She shuddered, captivated by the sudden animal sheen in them. She didn't need to lower her gaze to see that he stood naked before her. Her peripheral vision, though slightly fuzzy without her glasses, didn't miss the smooth, rippled, bare flesh, even in the dim light. No, this man's prowess had a way of perking up all the senses and stimulating new ones she didn't know she possessed.

Damn the cocky jerk.

"Huh?"

He tightened his grip and lowered her arm. "The lenses. They could be used as a fire-lighting tool. Since we don't know what resources we'll have or how long we'll be here, don't throw anything out. Got it?"

"Got it," she replied through clenched teeth. Yanking her wrist from his hand, she asked, "Would you please cover yourself with something?"

He looked down, then back up at her. Of course, she should have known her suggestion would tip him off. He grasped the knot at her breasts and yanked her toward him. Her body slammed against him, and even though the quilt served as a barrier, she could still feel the bulge of his manhood against her lower abdomen. Even more aware of it now than she had been by the sight of it, memories of it ripping into her with passion only hours ago racked her body.

He jerked and pulled until he had the knot untied. The cloth slipped from her in one motion. Despite the shock of it, of the balmy air caressing every inch of her skin, she stood her ground, this time not giving him the satisfaction of so much as a flinch.

His eyes flitted to hers momentarily, and if she wasn't mistaken, desire bloomed there as he moved his stare down the length of her. A small measure of retaliation, she decided, for he could look all he wanted, but he would no longer get to touch. His straight, white teeth glowed in the lunar light when he clamped the edge of the fabric between them and pulled downward in one smooth action. Soon, a tattered panel of the tan backing was peeled away. He wadded the remainder up and pushed it into her belly. She took it and watched as he fashioned himself a loincloth much like Tarzan might wear. With the moonlight spearing down on his sinewy build, and the new garment he wore now settled snug above corded, long legs, Jewel's pulse surged up to choke her.

"Better?" He jammed his fists on narrow hips.

No, much more devastating. "Ah...yes," she croaked. Swallowing a dry lump, she couldn't help but hone her gaze in on the thickness that swelled from beneath the garment. Her pussy throbbed anew and the beginning traces of want trickled onto her inner thighs. That's when she decided that naked would have been better. There was something about that uncivilized Tarzan look that proved lethal to her pride and determination to stave him off. So opposite from the well-groomed, well-mannered rogue she was more familiar with.

Trembling, she rewrapped the remains of the blanket around her body.

He turned. "Now watch your step this time. Follow me—and don't get lost, you hear?"

She didn't bother answering him. Though she'd give anything to be a thousand miles from him right now, he didn't have to force her to stay with him. The dark jungle surrounding them, coupled with the eerie sounds and sometimes-suspicious quiet within its depths, was enough to make her hug his heels. She forced herself to keep his sinewy back in her line of vision, for she could swear half a dozen twin pairs of glazed red eyes stared back at her throughout the dense brush.

He trekked through the thickness, batting away draped Spanish moss and leaping over fallen trees. She limped along behind him, her ankle throbbing with pain, and never took her eyes from that broad back. It seemed, she noted, that he headed toward the sound of the rushing surf and open territory. Jewel winced, every now and then stepping on a sharp object or protruding seashell. Long palmetto leaves sliced at her skin like a garden of machetes. Insects buzzed about her head, and she slapped at the relentless pests where they bit into her uncovered arms and legs. Sweat dribbled down between her breasts, pooled in her armpits and gathered on her brow and upper lip. Now in stark contrast to the Arctic they'd just endured, this place was absolutely sweltering! God, what she wouldn't do for a bath right about now.

She didn't know how much time had passed, six, maybe eight hours, perhaps? It seemed the jungle went on and on, never-ending, despite the constant sound of the surf looming ahead. Disoriented, irritable, tired, thoroughly parched and hungry, she battled with her own mind. Was this all a nightmare, or was it real? How could all these discomforts feel so real if they were only in her sleep-filled mind? Oddly, the sun seemed to be on a schedule of its own, and she wondered if it were day, night, winter or summer.

Finally, she could take it no more. "Vince."

He stopped and turned. His body glistened in the moonlight, the sweat shimmering diamonds on his finely cut frame.

Winded from both the sexy sight of him and the relentless journey, she panted, "I need to rest, to…to go behind the bushes."

He nodded, jutting his chin toward a cluster of small, immature pines. "Go there. I'll be able to keep an eye on you while still giving you your privacy. After you, I'll take a turn, and then we better keep moving. I can sense the shore up ahead."

It didn't take them long to take care of the necessities. By the time they resumed the hike and broke through the edge of the mangrove onto a beach set within a lagoon, she was stripping the thick quilt from her drenched body. The water called to her, lapping, crashing into the narrowed mouth of the cove and onto the private beach. She couldn't breathe, and desperately needed to feel the cool waters on her fiery skin. Tossing the broken glasses onto the pile of her torn and now filthy garment, she hobbled barefoot across the still-warm sand. The pain in her ankle became secondary to the immediate need for cooling relief. A blissful sigh escaped her when a balmy wind blew inland and ruffled her hair up and off her perspiring neck. It dried and cooled the ardor between her legs, making her long for nothing but the privacy of a refreshing dip in the water.

She could feel those eyes on her, branding her cooling flesh, but she didn't care. Jewel stepped into the lapping waves, ignoring the sting of saltwater upon her many scratches and abrasions. In heaven now, she kept walking until the water swallowed her whole and blessed relief cradled her from head to toe.

* * * * *

Vince stood glued to the sand. Spellbound, he watched as she shed the barrier and walked right into the surf. He thought of a voluptuous mermaid, her abundant breasts free and gleaming in the silver moonlight, her body transforming from full woman to half-creature with each step she took into the sea. The lunar light made the golden blonde of her medium-length hair shimmer with tiny jewels, crowning her, further emphasizing the mystique of this woman he never truly knew before arriving on this island. His gaze moved down the long length of her, tracing every cushy curve, every inlet. He visually caressed his name etched upon her ass. Hot blood rushed to his cock and he knew a desperate need to follow her into that revitalizing lair. His breath quickened and he smacked his lips, savoring the taste of her that still lingered in his mouth. Sweat poured down his face and chest. He longed to cool his flesh yet stoke his ardor at the same time.

He had her back. The mere thought of it overjoyed him with giddiness. She was here, in his life once again. For four long years, he'd endured that empty, lonely life of trying to convince himself his carefree existence without her was every man's dream. He'd been a lucky bastard to have all those women fawning over him—or so he'd insisted at the time. Vince snorted to himself. Well, that lifestyle of numb emotions and selfishness wasn't his any longer. His dream stood before him, a proud, beautiful siren of the sea. For the first time in his life he saw his future, he had direction. Direction that led him straight to her.

And he wasn't letting her or anyone else tell him otherwise.

To prove that little point to her, he waded in, ignoring the insistent pounding in his loins. He walked into deeper water until he stood chest-high in the bay. His sweat-beaded skin sizzled against the cool waters. The gentle waves lapped against him, almost lulling him with their comfort and weightless quality upon his body. Weary, tired bones and muscles relaxed as he waited for her to rise out of the water.

She broke the surface closer to shore, her face tipped toward the starlit sky so that her hair slicked back across her scalp. It left her heart-shaped face prominent and unframed for his perusal. She sighed her relief and opened her eyes at the same moment his breath clogged in his throat. Twin orbs of palm-frond green stared back at him in the moonlight.

"What?" She blinked the droplets from her eyes. "What are you looking at?"

"You." He turned and trudged toward her, never taking his gaze from her shocked expression.

"No!" A hand shot out of the water halting him. "Don't you come any closer. Stay away or I'll—"

She stumbled back into shallower water as he approached. Shaking her head frantically, she backed away from him, tripping on her own fear. She faltered, he knew with certainty, against her own temptations.

"Or you'll what, Jew—Jane?"

He delighted in the gasp his slipup tore from her depths, even though he'd vowed to himself to play along with her farce. The jarring mistake made her completely lose her footing. She tumbled backward so that she landed on her ass, the water at waist level.

"What did you call me?"

He neared, dropping to his knees as the water surface rose to surround his hips. Vince crawled toward her where she lay sprawled in shallow water, her eyes round moons of fear.

"Jane. I called you Jane. That's your name—isn't it?"

She swallowed audibly. Leaning back on her elbows, she pushed with her feet against the underwater sand, attempting to crabwalk out of his reach.

But he anticipated her tactic long before she'd executed it. Snatching her uninjured ankle under the water, he yanked her toward him so that she became pinned beneath him, unable to escape.

"Isn't it?" he asked again.

"Of course it is." She pushed against his unyielding chest. The scent of her warm, salty flesh filled his nostrils, driving him wild with a need to taste her. "Now get off me."

"Oh, I'm going to get off, all right. You can count on that, Jane." Relief washed over her face at his casual use of the fake name. Obviously, she'd convinced herself he still believed her to be Jane. Which suited him just fine for the time being.

Her dazed whimper barely had time to escape before his mouth descended on hers. She struggled against him, her muffled cry and thrashing limbs further inflaming him. He swept her mouth with his tongue while his hands gripped her wrists and held them pinned above her head. Water lapped around her, making her appear all the more mermaid-like. Jewel bucked against his weight, but her wild, angry groans soon turned to reluctant moans as he wiggled his hips in between her legs. Under the cool water, the tip of his cock brushed her hardened clit. She stilled her fight and slowly her legs relaxed and spread wide. He twined one hand around both of her wrists, freeing one of his own hands for exploration.

Tearing his mouth from hers, he rained kisses over her bowed neck and panted, "Why do you fight me? Why do you always say no when you really mean yes?"

"No..." she cried softly. "Please, you don't understand."

"Oh, I understand perfectly. You see, me Tarzan, you Jane." He filled his free hand with her swelling bosom and sucked a sea-bathed nipple between his lips. Warm, salty flavor burst in his mouth while his tongue dueled with the taut pebble. She arched against him, her cry of ecstasy rising up into the moon-glazed sky, out over the rush of the tide beyond the cove.

"And since you don't seem to want to face your own body's obvious desires, well, then...we'll have to go at it primitive-like." He snarled as he pushed aside the loincloth and aligned himself with her cunt. Alternating, she nodded and shook her head madly, as if a split personality battled in her head. "See? Indecisive female breed that you are, if you choose this route, I can be that jungle animal you secretly desire. I'll choose for you. I know you. I know what you really want, *Jane*."

"No—yes!" she screamed as he tore into her with the desperation of a wild beast. The fire of her passage made him shudder. The drastic change in temperature from the cool sea to her warm juices shocked him with blissful pleasure. He throbbed, nearly spilling his seed with the single motion of that one deep stroke.

"Tell me you want me." He had to hear it from her lips before he went any further. He kissed her with sudden tenderness, her mouth, her cheeks, her chin, even as he held her down with brutal force. The sexual rage eased from him when she lifted her head, chasing his mouth with hers. Her full breasts rose and fell with each ragged breath she took, sliding sensually against his naked chest. The song of lapping waves around their joined bodies surrounded them.

Finally, she nodded and whimpered. "I want you, Vince. I've always wanted you, damn it." She tore her wrists from his grip and stabbed her hands into his hair. Her legs clamped around him, imprisoning him in the trap of her womanhood. Even if he'd wanted to, there was no escaping her now. The primitive creature in her emerged, no longer the hunted, but the hunter. Her mouth found his with a rabid growl, the bittersweet flavor of sex still on her lips.

Jewel rammed her pelvis up against him, drowning his cock in her tightness. But carnal, animal instinct took over. She suddenly released her legs and pushed against him, rolling him over in the water. Still joined, she came over him, moaning her pleasure when her weight pushed him deeper inside her as she straddled him.

Looking up at her now, he thought of that sea siren. The full silver moon shone behind her head, crowning her with an ethereal glow. Behind him, the trees in the forest rustled in the balmy, coconut-scented breeze. His back lay against packed, wet sand while his rapid thrusts into her core caused the intermittent rise and fall of their joined bodies upon the incoming waves. Her breasts jiggled above him, the tight, knotted peaks dark candy morsels glistening in the night. He reached up and squeezed the fullness, twisting and pinching the nipples, further luring out the hidden animal in her.

Though she now dominated him by positioning herself on top, he remained in control. He saw who she was, knew it better than she did. She bounced on top of him, skimming her hands over first her body, then his, in an obvious frenzy of need. Her eyes went limpid and a guttural sound erupted from deep in her throat. That sticky canal tightened around his dick, and at that very second, she sucked in a breath and held it.

"I'm about to…"

"Oh, honey, yes. Let it out."

She threw her head back and howled to the moon. Her luscious body twitched around him. A ferocious uprising of lust overpowered him. He slapped his hands down on her hips and dug his fingers in, holding her in place as his balls exploded. Erupting with a force to rival that of a volcano, his deep moan rose just as her cry died out. She collapsed upon his chest, and even though cool water surrounded him, his flesh burned in celebration at having her back in his arms again.

He gathered her close and glanced over her shoulder. Petting her back, he rubbed his palms over the moist, soft texture of her sea-soaked skin. Squinting, he gazed up at the moon—and swore he saw a raven-black, winged horse glide across the cratered surface carrying a man and woman.

But there wasn't time to study it further. Jewel's sobs drew his eyes back to Earth. The gulps started off soft, almost indiscernible, and escalated to full-blown wails.

"What...what's wrong, babe?" He cupped her face and lifted her head so that he could look into her face. And what he saw there startled him. It far surpassed the emotion he'd seen the night she'd come to him with the marriage ultimatum. Her eyes glittered with a frightening mixture of torment and anger. The lips that only moments ago had devoured him with hunger, now tightened with restraint as she fought to suppress hiccups of pain. Every muscle in her body stiffened.

And without warning, she ripped herself from him. His cock jolted against the assault as cold water rushed around him. "What the hell?"

She leaped to her feet and marched from the shallow water. He swiveled his head, blinking as water sprayed his face. Watching her retreat, bafflement kept him floating there, speechless at the sudden change of mood.

"You bastard!" She bent and snatched up the blanket, presenting him with the luscious angle of her slit. "Don't you *ever* do that to me again. Do you hear me? Huh? Do you *hear* me?"

He sighed, dragging himself up to a standing position. "So, we're back to that, are we?"

"So, we're back to that, are we?" she mimicked, snapping the sand from the cloth. With adept precision, she swirled it around her body and secured it with a knot at her breasts. Tattered now from their long journey through the jungle, it dragged the ground behind her in a train of torn scraps. His gaze moved lower to the legs that peeped out as she walked. And his eyes widened in disbelief.

"Why didn't you tell me about that?" He waded from the water.

She followed the path of his stare and flipped the edge of the quilt over the wide, oozing gash on her ankle. "It's none of your business," she snarled.

"Jesus, woman, it's going to get infected if you don't do something with it."

She crossed her arms over her abdomen and sauntered right up to him, accidentally brushing his lower abdomen as she did so. Awareness of her smell, her heat, even her remembered taste, burst in his brain. Looking up, she spit twin darts of fire at him. Tears had been replaced by a new more noble cause.

"And why, may I ask, do you care if I get an infection?" Before he could reply, she held up a hand. "No. Don't say a word. I already know the answer." And she spun, leaving him in a cloud of her sexual scent tinged with hot anger.

"Oh really?" He snatched up her broken glasses she'd left behind in her rage and followed right on her trail. "What *is* my answer?"

"Well, that's obvious, isn't it?" She threw it over her shoulder as she followed a bend in the lagoon and moved on out toward the open shoreline. "As usual, you care only for yourself. So, if I should come down with an affliction, it's not amenable to your prowess. You don't get to take advantage of me anymore." Her eyes widened as she whirled on him. "Oh, wait," she said with sudden false cheer. Her grin spread wide and sarcastic upon her exquisite, moonlit face. "I'm totally wrong, aren't I? You'll probably attack me anyway, whether I'm sick or not, just like you've been doing ever since we got shoved into this fucking nightmare."

Now he knew she was beyond pissed. "Fuck" was a word she never used unless highly provoked. But goddamn it, he was pissed, too!

"Attack, you say?"

The briefest flicker of wariness lit her eyes right before she turned and stalked away. "Yes, attack."

"That's a damn lie and you know it." He fell into step beside her.

"Is not."

He snatched her elbow and hauled her around to face him. In a flash of frustration, he had her in his arms. Carefully controlled, he executed the most devastating, gentle, passion-filled kiss he could muster. She melted against him with a strained cry of surrender. Her fists bunched into the fabric of his loincloth. A slow curl of renewed awareness washed through him, from the softness of her breasts pressed to his chest, all the way down to her trembling legs buckling against his.

Damn if he wasn't getting a hard-on again. But this wasn't the time. *You're proving a point here, Vince. Don't forget it, or you'll lose ground with the wishy-washy, wily fox.*

He moved his hands up slowly to her jaw and pulled her mouth from his. The stunned, drugged glaze in her eyes was all the proof he needed for them both. "Now, do you call *that* an unwanted attack?"

Her eyes narrowed even as she panted. She stepped out of his arms and started to raise her hand to him. But the sudden flare of the sun had her halting her assault. The moon and starlit darkness had disappeared. As if a light switch had once again been flipped, an azure sky materialized above them, filled with the glowing ball of a high-noon sun. Temperatures soared, baking them in an oven of sweltering heat.

Jewel swayed as sweat beaded on her brow. "Oh shit." She plopped to the sand and groaned, holding her head in her hands. "What now?"

"I don't know." He collapsed and stretched out next to her, one arm thrown across his eyes to shield the bright rays of the sun. "But it's hotter than the fricking desert, and I'm dying of thirst and hunger."

Her stomach growled. "Me too. So now what, Tarzan? Got any big, bright, manly ideas?"

"Shh, I'm thinking."

"Do we just give ourselves up to the sea, or call for help from those *stupid* genies?"

He peeped at her from under his forearm. "Goddamn it, Jane, watch your mouth. We don't know what they're capable of."

Chapter Six

Luke guided the skiff past the cove toward the slight peninsula. "No, they really don't know what we're capable of, do they, my lovely…?"

He paused, still unable to assimilate this Jennie with the one he knew and loved. Now in old-hag, witchy form, she had the power to render him speechless by a mere glance. She wore a wide-brimmed straw hat atop scraggly, gray-streaked black hair that hung in stringy ropes down her hunched back. Her gnarled hands sported long, curled fingernails. Wrinkled skin sagged loose beneath various large-stone rings that winked in the sunlight. On her bony little body drooped a ragged, faded gingham dress from many eras past. He shuddered, relieved the wart-riddled honker, rotten teeth and green-toned skin weren't real.

"What's the matter, honey?" Her voice even gave him the willies. Whiskey-roughened and hovering just short of a screech, he sure didn't want it whispering in his ear during lovemaking. "Black cat got your tongue?"

She cackled, raising her pocked face to the sky as they skimmed along the water. Her voice carried out over the hum of the motor and into the bay as they passed by, scattering a school of wading sea gulls. They cawed in fright as they fluttered into the forest and took cover in a group of date palms.

He glanced toward the shore and steered the bow of the craft toward the small pier. "I'm sorry, Jennie, but I just can't stomach you like that."

She growled low in her throat, and he thought of a hissing black feline on Halloween. "And you think I can stand the sight of you, dear?"

He looked down at himself. At first, the transformation she'd insisted on had scared the crap out of him. Emaciated and void of muscle, he'd been altered drastically to look like her exact male counterpart. It even seemed, he thought as he bumped the stern against the dock and shut the motor down, that he'd lost every ounce of his strength. The thought of being permanently weak and ugly scared him shitless and did frightening things to his ego.

"Eh, can we just get this little lesson over with? I'd really prefer to go back to having an erect cock as opposed to full-body aches and stiffness." He rubbed his back, tied off the craft and hobbled over the low bench seat. Reaching out a scrawny hand, he assisted her unsteadily up to the pier.

Jennie snorted, very unladylike. He climbed up on shaky limbs and stood next to her. She gazed into his eyes, and gratefully, he saw the beauty of her there inside those amber depths. "Master, I second that. Even now, my wrinkled old pussy is getting wet just thinking about your shriveled up *phallus* spearing me."

Vince gulped. His stomach churned. "Jennie. Please."

With a toss of her head, she let out a nasally cackle and crossed to the couple who lay on the beach baking in the sun she'd just set into force.

She sobered and slanted him a scolding look. "Luke, we've got a job to do here. It includes easing into character when needed."

"Yes, you're right, sweetheart. And in this case, it's definitely needed. That woman is more stubborn than an entire pack of mules."

"True," she replied, hobbling through the sand. "But your old college friend there has a bit more work to do, himself. Not nearly as much as Jewel, but he has been unknowingly instrumental in the hardening of her heart. It is now our job to boost along the thawing that has already begun in her soul—er, uh, in her libido, more accurately. But alas! They both need help, and we've come to the rescue. I only hope..."

Luke knew that tone well. He gripped her arm gently and turned her, halting her in her painful gait. "Jennie? What is it? What do you hope?"

She looked over Luke's shoulder at the couple who just now took note of their arrival. "I only hope they can accept their love for one another by the end of the three days. We now near the completion of day one."

"And if they don't?"

A tear formed in the wrinkled corner of her eye. "They will live on in loneliness and never know the depth of love and carnality we feel for one another. And I could risk my sister, Queen Justina, banishing me back to the bottle—without you."

"No." He gasped it out. Luke had thought all the danger had passed for them. Her almighty Xanthian sister had ordained Jennie as the honorable Goddess of Carnality after she'd completed her feat of the thirteen orgasms. Her mission and fate with Luke had been honorably concluded—thanks to his help—and already encrypted as a hidden destiny in *The Book of Xanthus*. So naturally, he'd thought they'd be living a carefree eternity on his hedonist island bringing people together in love and lust.

Without further threat of being forced apart.

"Yes." She looked up at him, and through the hideous face, he saw his love with crystal clarity. "This is a serious job we've been given, Luke. We must never take its goal or one another for granted. Ever."

She turned then and tottered away, and Luke knew a fierce love and devotion like never before. He would make Vince and Jewel see the error of their ways; he would make them love one another if he had to tie them up together for the rest of their lives.

* * * * *

"Well it's about time." Jewel sat up and watched the old crones shuffle toward them. Their tiny little hunched-over bodies didn't concern her. She'd caught sight of their boat. Which meant transportation back to the mainland.

"What?" Vince propped himself up on one elbow, shielding his eyes from the glaring sun.

"An old couple's coming up the beach. Must be fishermen. They have a boat—we're going home, Vince!"

"I...where? I don't see a boat."

"Right...there..." She leapt to her feet and stood on tiptoe, straining to see around the elderly couple. "But...but I saw it, I swear I did. I even *heard* it, didn't you?" She turned to look down at him, demanding an answer she knew she wouldn't be getting. Obviously, he'd been napping and hadn't heard or seen a thing.

"All I see," he amended as he rose, "is the old couple. No boat." He dismissed her as if she'd suffered heat-induced hallucinations, and strode forward. "Hello! And where did you fine folks come from? Taking an afternoon stroll up the beach?"

The hag slowed her steps and turned, fisting the neckline of her ragged dress when the wind whipped around her. She raised one silver brow. "Strolling? Eh! If you want to call it that."

"Been 'strolling' for decades trying to find our way home." That from the old man. His stooped body, stiff gray mop of hair and tissue-paper skin told Jewel he wouldn't be strolling much longer.

"For decades?"

"Oh yes, lass." The woman shuffled across the sand leaving behind a pair of long ruts. She approached and Jewel got a potent whiff of body odor and foul breath. Her eyes snared Jewel, pale gold swimming in tanned leather wrinkles above sagging jaws. A shiver raced up Jewel's spine when those eyes blurred and appeared to turn to the very color of her own, as if she looked at a reflection of her future self. "Put here by a pair of dim-witted genies way back when we was a-young'uns, mm-hm, that we were," she nodded, smacking her lips.

The old man chuckled, followed by a fit of coarse coughs. "Oh yeah. But it's all her fault. Stubborn old witch, she is. Caused us to be damned to this place forever, and all because she ain't got sense to just face what's deep inside her."

"Shut up, you old bastard!" The hag turned on him, snarling, as murderous hate gleamed in her eyes. They'd turned back to pale brown, Jewel noted, and she briefly wondered if she'd imagined seeing herself in the woman's gaze. "Ha! Ignore the damn geezer. Always blamin' me when *he's* the one who wouldn't give in to fate all those years ago. I'm just reactin' to his obstinate ass. You see?"

"I see." Vince merely stood back and studied the two, his arms folded with guardedness.

"Yeah, um, we get it." Weirdoes, Jewel thought.

"Now ya happy? They got it, ya old crone." He continued on, sidestepping the pounding surf. "Let's keep a-movin', keep on with this never-ending stalemate."

The woman nodded and started out after him. But she paused and turned then, boring her eyes into Jewel. Hobbling forward, she grasped a long silver chain that hung around her skinny neck. Unfastening it from her nape, she hooked its ends together and reached up, placing it over Jewel's head. A ruby-encrusted, two-inch-long key dangled from the thick chain and nestled into her cleavage above the knotted quilt. It twinkled in the sunlight, the silver shining as if it had been recently polished.

"What...what are you doing?" Jewel ran her fingertips along the smooth edges, the sharp stones. Warm, soothing vibrations shimmied up her arm.

"Giving you the key to your heart." She smiled then, a mass of grooves and pocked flesh. "I cain't seem to use it to find mine. Hopefully, you'll have better luck than I did."

Jewel glanced at Vince, then back at the woman. The old man was already ten yards up shore. "Well, I...I thank you — ma'am."

"Eh! You thank yourself when you find your way off this blasted island. We never could, but hopefully, you two will..."

"Are you saying we could be here indefinitely?" Vince's voice held a trace of irritation and panic, which caused the heavy dread in Jewel's abdomen to tighten.

The woman's eyes riveted to him. She crossed then, to stand so that she looked up at him. The contrast made Jewel think of a giant looking down upon an elf. She removed a ring from one gnarled finger, its wide silver band winking by the rays of the sun. With a tremor of weakness, she reached out and clutched Vince's large hand. Though the ring had just been removed from her bony index finger, it slid onto his finger with ease and fit as if it had been made for him.

"The key to my heart?" he asked her, a sardonic grin on his handsome face.

She nodded and stepped away. "Aye, the key to your heart. Now, I must be on my way. This island isn't getting any smaller, you know."

With a tottering gait, she turned and followed the old man. He vanished first beyond a bend in the shoreline. Within a minute, so did she.

"What the hell do you suppose *that* was all about?" Jewel held the key in her hand, the chain still around her neck. Tearing her eyes from the spot where the couple had last been seen, she turned the key this way and that, studying its intricate, antique pattern.

Vince twisted the ring around his finger, still staring up the beach. "I have my suspicions." He shrugged. "But who knows. Probably just a couple of loons."

"Well, now what? Do we keep the jewelry?"

He spun and strode into the dense woods. "Yes, we keep them. In this situation, we keep everything, because you never know what might come in handy later. And we keep going, too, just like the old couple."

They followed the shoreline just into the edge of the forest. For what seemed hours, she trailed along behind him, batting aside the drooping limbs and moss. As the minutes and hours crept by, her mouth became a pit of dry, parched sand. The scent of her own sweat permeated the balmy, stifling air around her nostrils, while streams of moisture dribbled down her back and chest. Her entire body ached, and she talked herself out of the vague waves of nausea that started to plague her belly. The aroma of cassia carried heavy on the damp air edged by the faint odor of soil.

"God, what I wouldn't do for an ice-cold bottle of water."

Vince finally pushed through a tangled mass of vines. He stopped so abruptly she nearly crashed into his back. "Well, I can't guarantee there'll be water inside, but it looks like we've found new shelter."

"Oh, thank—what?" She stepped around him and looked up at the massive structure. "Oh my God. It's a giant tree house."

"On the ground, in a tree, in the sky." He crossed the small clearing to the base of the massive trunk. "I don't really care anymore. I just want shelter, a place to rest and a home base for a chance to go hunt up some water and food."

He tested the strength of the bamboo ladder and, satisfied, climbed upward until he reached a trap door. Grunting, he flipped it inward and glanced down at her. "You coming?"

Jewel tore her gaze from the rippling tan sheen of his body. His raven-dark hair stood wild and mussed upon his head. With the loincloth tied around his narrow hips, he appeared every bit the jungle man, primal and fierce. In that instant, her heart fluttered with a primitive need that forced a violent shudder through her. Flames smoldered in her loins, heating her juices to the boiling point.

She swallowed, struggling to catch her breath. "Coming? Um, yes, of course."

Inside, the structure was about the size of her confined room at the convent. She noted one hinged window on each wall, and a pitched, bamboo-beamed ceiling covered with thatching. The windows were closed to the high tree branches and sultry heat. Other than those few openings, Jewel determined, the door they'd just crawled through appeared to be the only entrance. She looked about and took in the few stacked crates along one matting-covered wall. Next to them were several corked bottles and jugs, and two hammocks tied to centrally located bamboo poles.

Relief washed through her, but it came tinged with a faint stab of disappointment at the sleeping arrangements. Crossing to the crates, she opened the first one, set before her on the slatted wood floor. Peering in, she sifted through various toiletry items. She eyed the shampoo and toothbrush with longing. *Thank you, Luke.* With a grateful sigh, she closed the lid and moved on to the next chest.

"What do we have inside?" He knelt and worked on the rusted lock of another trunk.

"The one over there contains some much-needed toiletries, soap, toothpaste, stuff like that. And this one..." She groaned. "Is empty."

"Let's pray there's food in one of them. I'm so damned starved, I could eat a whale." He wiggled the latch loose and raised the lid. Hinges squeaked, grating against Jewel's eardrums. A musty cloud rose to assault her senses.

"Empty, too." In a frantic rush, he opened another, then another. The final chest inspected, he slammed the lid shut, clapped the dust from his palms and stood. Hands on hips, he moved around the room. "Looks like all we have to eat is fucking shaving cream."

"No…" She fell back on her rear. "This can't be. It just can't. I-I need water, food, I…"

"Jane!"

Her head snapped up. She watched as he bent down on his haunches and grasped her ankle. The slight touch nearly made her jump out of her skin. "Ouch!"

"Your ankle. Why didn't you tell me it's gotten worse?" He scanned it, this time moving his head rather than her foot. "It's red, swollen"—he pressed his fingertips to the large pink circle surrounding the wound—"and hot. And there's pus coming from it."

"It's fine." She wrestled her ankle from his strong grip.

"Goddamn it, it's not fine. It's infected." He raked a hand through his damp hair. She caught the brief scent of sweat and powerful man. "You need a doctor."

Lord help her, but she couldn't withstand the light of concern in his eyes. It made her ache with soppy sentiment. She longed to fly into his arms, to let him coddle and soothe the pain that snaked up her leg right into her heart.

"I *said* I'm fine." She slapped his hand away. "Now please go find some water."

He pressed a hand to her forehead. His eyes lit with a compassion she almost believed. "Jane, you're on fire. You need a cool bath, some medicines…or something."

He doesn't really care, Jewel. Remember that. He just loathes the idea of being left all alone on a deserted island.

She tried to prevent her nostrils from flaring, tried to suppress the sudden sarcastic dart of her eyes. "Ah, well, hold on one moment. I'll just go grab some penicillin from the medicine cabinet and—"

"Stop it." He was already opening the windows to let in the breeze, and unfastening one of the hammocks from the poles. He took it, folding it this way and that, and laid it upon the floor like a mattress.

"Take off the blanket and lay down."

She groaned. "Oh, we're back to you bullying me, are we?"

He pressed his lips together, setting his hands carefully upon his hips. With his legs spread apart, and the backdrop of the jungle behind him through the open window, she imagined a lion standing beside him with ferocious devotion. The cleft in his square jaw only added to the aura, and she imagined kissing the dip, or feeling the rough stubble there drag across her inner thighs. She sighed inwardly as a warm, gooey flood of excitement settled between her legs. Yes, he certainly exuded the image of the mighty king of the jungle, potent, supreme…sexy.

"You have a fever. If you keep that thick blanket around you, I'll be burying you in the sand. Now. I said. Take. That. Damn. Thing. Off!"

A thrill raced through her blood and did a flip-flop deep inside her belly. His eyes gleamed murderously. Every muscle in his body flexed with tension and near rage as he braced himself for her defiance.

But she didn't feel like fighting him. Come to think of it, she mused, pressing a hand to her forehead, she *was* feeling lousy. She wouldn't mind lying down for a bit. Her head pounded, her body seemed to roast within the blanket's confines and that vague nausea plagued her. If only she could have some water, just a smidgen.

Obediently, she crossed to the makeshift bed, unfastened the quilt and let it fall to the floor. Vince's swift intake of breath filled her ears with joy. But she made no indication. Kneeling, she collapsed onto the bed and sighed. Within seconds, her eyelids fluttered shut and she welcomed the cool realm of blessed darkness.

* * * * *

He shook her gently. "Jane."

Her eyes fluttered open. Fatigued, bloodshot pools of emerald stared back at him. "What?" she rasped.

"I'm going to go hunt up some food and water. Okay?"

She nodded, rolling onto her side. He swept her curvy, naked body with an appreciative look. "Go back to sleep. I'll be back soon." Surprisingly, she obeyed, giving into the exhaustion once again.

Confident she wasn't in a coma, Vince blew out a breath of sheer relief. The long hours of fighting their way through the thick foliage had obviously taken its toll on her. Coupled with the infection in the wound, the sweltering, long journey they'd taken had been just enough to weaken her into submission. And given the circumstances, he'd much rather see her fighting back than giving up.

He climbed down the ladder and scanned the perimeter. First to procure water. Though Jewel had no clue about his past experience, and would like to think otherwise, Vince was no idiot when it came to survival techniques. He shook his head as he trekked through a dense thicket. No, it hadn't always been champagne, caviar and pâté for him. Long before meeting her, he'd served a four-year tour in the military. Special Operations forces were expected and trained to endure the harshest of climates. Sure, those leisurely years since his honorable discharge had made him a bit rusty, but no properly trained man forgot the basics of those survival tools that were ingrained into him without mercy.

"Bingo." He spotted the cluster of green bamboo plants. But first, he needed a cutting tool of some sort. Searching through a barren area of rock and sand, he spotted a shiny protrusion. He knelt and dug around it, careful to avoid its sharp edges.

The sand piled around him, Vince sat back on his haunches and gaped at the object. "Two pieces of iron? Buried in the sand on a deserted island?" He raised his gaze to the darkening sky. "Jennie, if this is your doing, why not just *poof* and give me a saw and a nice big machete?"

A breeze blew in, partially drying the glaze of sweat covering his body. With it came her scent, soft and seductive. He heard a distant tinkling sound, but Jennie refused to materialize.

"Ah, so you're trying to teach me a lesson? See how good I am at caring for her on my own? Or are you just being stubborn and delighting in our desperate situation?"

An angry rumble roared in the distance. It wasn't thunder, but the wrath of a touchy genie.

He pulled the long metal pieces from the grave and held them up for inspection. Glints of sunlight reflected from their surface. Just perfect, he thought, to shape a saw and a long hunting knife. Locating a large flat boulder as a metalworking station, he then searched for rock that could be used as a hammer.

It took him the good part of an hour to shape the tools into useful, jagged cutting edges. The ping and grind of rock against metal satisfied and worked out much of his tension.

And he worked with her in mind, her safety, her health, her comfort and happiness.

As he tied off the ends, fashioning handles with hardwood wrapped snug by the shaggy material found at the base of sugar palm leaves, he realized it had always been so. Jewel had walked out on him, but he'd never stopped hoping for her happiness. He'd never quite rid himself of the hope that someday he'd see her again. Someday he'd be able to make her happy once again.

He held up the knife and studied its sharp edge. Running his finger along the blade, he drew a line of blood. "Perfect."

Vince made his way back to the thicket of green bamboo. Lopping off the tops of several shoots, he bent them over, securing the ends with palm fronds so that water began to drip from the raw top opening. Ripping off several cocoyam leaves from a cluster nearby, he shaped them into bowls and placed them below the droplets.

Wiping his perspiring brow with the back of his wrist, he mumbled, "From these, we'll have water by tomorrow."

Quickly now, he gathered several green coconuts that had rolled from the base of a nearby towering palm. They would provide just enough liquid to get them through the night. The bamboo source would give them enough for cooking by tomorrow. Later, he'd have to locate a banana or plantain tree for an instant and abundant source of water. The saw he'd made would come in handy for cutting down these valuable trees. Once cut, it would only be a matter of scooping out the center of the stump and allowing the bowl-shaped hollow to fill with water from the roots. Each tree could theoretically provide them with up to four days of a good water source. But finding the tree could prove difficult, since so far, he hadn't seen one single banana tree.

Holding the coconuts in the crook of one arm, he whacked at the heavy growth of vegetation, making an open path back toward the tree house. Insects buzzed incessantly around his head and wildlife scurried as he disrupted their habitats. He heard the nearby rush of the surf, the pleasant song of the cockatoos fluttering about in the tree branches and peaceful, primitive silence.

Vince came to the sudden conclusion that this nightmare he'd been placed in wasn't quite so bad. *Because of it, she was finally back in his life.*

The thought overjoyed him and got him thinking in a surprising direction. He determined that he was perfectly capable of providing for them. But the thought of it had him chuckling. She would certainly *love* that, he mused sarcastically, skirting around a poisonous rosary pea vine. What would life be like with her for the rest of their lives, forced to endure one another on this island? Would she always be difficult to live with, toxic like the red and black potent seeds of that rosary pea weed? The thought of being sentenced to her company for life, just as the old crones were with one another, intrigued him, and a pleasant swirl of contentment spun in his gut. A vision of her soft curves and snapping green eyes came to mind. Yes, he could certainly find contentment here with her, but there would never be a dull moment.

The tree house came into view, looming heavy yet partially camouflaged by the thick branches of the towering fig tree it perched in. It was then that he caught sight of the flowering fedegoso tree just behind their shelter. His heart stopped; his pulse burst in his throat on a sigh. The leaves of this medicinal tree were just what he'd been on the lookout for, just what he needed to concoct a brewed substance that could be applied to Jewel's wound to fight infection and ease pain. Relief flooded his system. He hadn't wanted to think what could have occurred if the infection had spread into her bloodstream.

"Thank you, Luke and Jennie," he breathed, closing his eyes.

The wind rustled gently, and with it a temporary burst of cold air and the sharp scent of the fedegoso's blooms.

You're very welcome.

* * * * *

She awoke to a delicious aroma…was that roast pork she smelled? Her stomach growled in answer and she stretched, prepared to go investigate. Wincing as her aching muscles protested, she opened her eyes and glanced around.

No, she wasn't waking up from the nightmare. She still lived it. And she remained in the tree house—still lying on that folded-up hammock on the hard, uneven slat of boards.

She combed a hand through her hair, fluttered it down over her cheek and neck. Perspiration no longer drenched her flesh. She felt cool to the touch, the fever gone. And she was famished!

Pressing a palm to her bare belly, she gasped when awareness flooded her senses. Jewel raised her head and studied her body, now adorned in a two-piece garment. Her breasts were cupped and tied by a torn piece of cloth from the quilt. It spread up and over each swell and fastened behind her neck in halter-top fashion. A short little swatch of the same fabric covered her hips, and the skirt resembled the loincloth Vince had worn. Understanding slammed into her with a pleasant mix of shock and excitement. How she'd gotten dressed this way could only be due to one thing, one person. *Him.* A sudden torrent of heat spread through her veins, settling between her legs. He'd touched her in her sleep. He'd studied and dressed her naked body during her exhausted nap.

And he'd… She moved her gaze down her exposed legs, lifting one to study her ankle. He'd doctored her infected wound. Drawing up her knee, she cautiously touched the dressing made from scraps of the blanket. A cream of some sort soaked through the strip. She smelled her fingertip and inhaled the fragrant yet medicinal aroma of the clear substance. Whatever it was, whatever he'd done to her, had made her feel better, revived and alive. The thought of his gentle hands on her as she slept, his caring ministrations, brought a swift surge of need to her that could only be quenched by one thing, one person.

Vince Santiago.

Sitting up, she crawled over to the corner set with the open hatch in the floor. Black stars filled her head as she up-righted herself to stand on the ladder. She took deep breaths and waited for the dizziness to pass. Once she had her bearings, she climbed down into an area that had been expertly readied into a habitable camp. With pleasant surprise, she noted he'd tidied the immediate campground area by clearing brush to make room for an outdoor area to dine and take leisure.

A wild boar roasted over a fire, speared in the kabob method and strung across the licking flames. Nearby, she saw her broken lenses and wondered if they'd come into play, allowing the fire to be sparked by the sun's magnification through their thickness. Jewel ran a hand across her brow. She hadn't worn the glasses since they'd broken, and still, he hadn't recognized her. As long as she continued to hold that anonymity trump card, he could toss them in the sea for all she cared.

Inhaling, she closed her eyes and drank in the delicious aroma. The scent of ham filled her nostrils almost intense enough to feed her by smell alone. She opened her lids and squinted, bringing the distant objects into focus. Across the site, a flat boulder had apparently become a countertop of sorts. Spread with an abundance of bananas, figs, oranges and various green food plants, it made her mouth water. Her gaze moved to a spot where the hot Florida sun bathed split coconuts set out to render coconut oil for cooking, and to help devise torches. Beyond that, a banana tree laid on its side, having been sawed down, its stump holding a basin of clear water from the roots. She marveled at the fact that she'd just discussed with her students, these very survival methods and foodstuff in the wild. It was as if a tiny little fairy—Luke or Jennie, perhaps?—had whispered in her ear, prompting her for her own future use to form a lesson plan about the tropics and enduring its harsh conditions.

How long had she slept, for God's sake? He'd transformed a jungle into a welcoming cozy home for them. Fuzzy, warm sentiment that had no right being there, oozed into her pounding heart. Hungrily, her eyes searched for him.

And her heart stopped beating, suspended in her chest along with the sharp intake of breath. She didn't need her glasses to sense the detailed glory of him.

He stood beneath a rose apple tree, a wild native of the jungle. In his hand, he held a long twine of braided palm husks, which split into three ropelike lengths. Upon each end, stones had been tied. Vince swung the bola above him, his muscles flexing as the cords whistled around his head. Snapping it with expert precision, he hit his target, tumbling dozens of pale red apples at his feet.

She watched as he bent and gathered them in his arms, tossing the rotten ones into the thick forest. His body glistened with the sweat of a hard day's work. Jewel longed to skim her hands over the expanse of chest, down along the length of his back, down to cup the firm rear hidden beneath the loincloth. He turned then, and she got a potent view of the bulge beneath the garment. A powerful yearning slammed into her with a vengeance. Her clit throbbed, pumping her womb full of intense need. Wet spurts of her own juice soaked her pussy lips, readying them for what she suddenly knew would happen.

And it would happen now.

Jewel, he doesn't want you for life, you've already determined that long ago. But he wants Jane for the here and now. Take it while you can get it. Savor him while you can. Go to him!

She ignored the slight twinge of pain in her ankle as she glided slowly across the clearing. And Jewel disregarded the hunger that plagued her stomach. Instead, she went to slake another, more insistent yearning. Above her, bright cockatoos and parakeets sang their high-pitched songs and fluttered from treetop to treetop. But Jewel didn't notice, didn't care. Even as the salt-scented sea breeze carried in over the jungle and swirled down around her, she paid no heed to the cooling sensation of it upon her bared limbs. The soles of her feet were pricked by sharp, patchy foliage as she walked, scorched by the hot sand, but the stimulus did not reach her besotted brain. Her vision, even without the aid of her glasses, came into clear focus as she neared. But she didn't need prescription lenses to tell her what her heart saw without a doubt.

Vince. He was all she could see, hear, smell, taste, feel. At one point in her life, she thought as she walked toward him, he'd been her entire world. She couldn't have things back the way they'd been, back when she'd *thought* he loved her—that she accepted. But she could certainly have him now in a different world, while he lasted, while this dream lasted. With each step she took, her eyes bored into him. She summoned him, drew his soul to hers with every ounce of mind power she had. Finally, his head snapped toward her, the arrows of his gaze piercing their surprising target. Her.

"Jane?" He dropped the apples. They rolled away in a shower of red. "Are you all right?"

"Make love to me," she breathed. "Now."

He blinked, cleared his throat. His body stiffened, as if he'd dragged in a breath he'd never be able to release.

When she stopped toe-to-toe before him, the scent of clean sweat and salty flesh filled her lungs. He must have taken a refreshing dip in the ocean, she mused, studying the slicked-back, sleek dark hair. Jewel longed to feel its thickness tangled in her fingers, to guide his head to her breast, down along her abdomen, to her core. The mental image of it sent a slow, thick curl of lust through her veins. She looked up into eyes as wide and dark as sin. The shock there thrilled her even more so than the sight of his gorgeous body. It told her all she needed to know.

He sighed as if an explanation had occurred to him, and pressed a hand to her forehead. "You're still running a fever, aren't you?"

"I have a fever all right," she agreed, twining her arms around his neck. "But it's between my legs."

He alternated pressing both hands front and back to her forehead, her neck, her cheeks. His face went pale. "You're cool. You're…you're not running a fever anymore."

Unable to wait for his disbelief to pass, she reached up, gripped one of his hands and slid it slowly down her chest, down along her torso, straight to the damp spot between her legs. The heat of his fingers against her bare, wet sex made her gasp before she replied on a pant, "I told you…" She kissed the cleft in his chin, swirled her tongue around in its depth, just as she'd longed to do when she'd first seen him again on the beach. "The fever's between my legs."

"Oh wow." He gulped. His body went rigid against hers. He let out a long groan when she encouraged him to take her, guiding his fingers over her, into her. Her legs twitched beneath her. She clung to his neck, spreading her stance, welcoming the heavy heat that swelled around his fingers.

"Ah, yes!" The uninhibited feline purr that escaped her throat empowered her with further confidence and bravery. But nothing gave her more encouragement than the instant, lusty glaze in his chocolate eyes. She stood on tiptoe and caught his bottom lip between her teeth as he pumped her pussy with three thick digits. "Yes, Vince. Yes. Just like that."

"Jesus…" He ripped his fingers from her, the bola now wrapped in a tangle around his free hand. With hurried speed and precision, he hitched her up so that he stood with her straddling his hips. "What's gotten into you?"

Her arms twined tighter around his neck. She tightened her legs about him, shoving the hem of her skirt up to circle her waist. It bared her entire vee and drew his gaze down so that he could see the pearly wetness of her lips. Warm sultry air caressed her tender flesh. The fragrance of her juices wafted up to tempt them both. Moaning, she ground her cunt over the soft fabric of his loincloth.

"Take me now, here." She couldn't breathe. The hot sun scorched their slick skin. Impatient, she ripped her top off in one swipe. Sweat poured down Vince's chest and off his brow, down onto her nipples. The erotic sensation of the warm droplets dousing her hot, taut nipples made her cry out, "Please, hurry…"

He stumbled several steps across the clearing. She didn't even notice the jolt of the fall when he lurched forward and they landed on the boulder. Fruit and leafy vegetables scattered off the rock, tumbling toward the roasting pig. With her legs spread, she raised her hips against his. Quickly, she yanked a large orange from behind her where it had wedged at the small of her back.

Tearing the peel from the round ball, she rasped, "Get your cock out. Now."

He didn't argue. With an impatient yank, he snatched the loincloth from his hips. Her breath caught when the long girth of him sprang free. Intermittent spears of sunlight shot down through the trees overhead, illuminating his penis in glory. The head was already swollen, the shaft almost fully hard. Jewel caught sight of the small pearl of pre-cum juice oozing from the slit. The rim tapered down into the long, veiny length of pure male organ. She continued to peel the orange as she devoured the sight of his erect shaft, her mouth watering with need. Her pussy muscles tightened, aching to be filled by that masterpiece.

But first she had to taste him. The orange fully peeled now, she sat up and gripped his penis with her free hand. Its satiny-covered steel more than filled her palm, and she delighted in the hiss her ministrations elicited from him. She looked at her other hand, shoved a thumb down into the center hole where the wedges all met, parting it so that the fruit spread for her.

Licking her lips, Jewel looked up at him where he stood bathed by the Florida sun. "I'm thirsty. I'm hungry. So hold still." And she held the orange between the cup of her palms, pushing downward until it ringed him, the wedges bursting apart, spreading like a flower's bloom around him. He moaned in blissful agony. She ignored the tensing of his body and cradled him so that the broken orange segments remained around him. The head of his rod barely peeped through the hole, tempting her with a rabid hunger.

Opening her mouth wide, she took him in along with the fruit. Tangy juice squirted out, dribbling down her chin and onto his balls. She tasted the bitter drop of cum, and swirled her tongue around the head while she pumped the sticky orange up and down his cock. The scent of citrus warmed by arousal fueled her senses. Her pussy seeped with its own sap, readying her passage for the coming onslaught of primal release.

He growled and snarled as a jungle cat might, ferocious and wild. She worked him hard, slathering up the juice and pulp, swallowing each and every drop. Sweet flavor burst in her mouth, feeding her crazed libido. Famished, she slurped, licked, nibbled. And when the fruit finally disappeared, she cupped his balls and licked them clean, stroking the hidden marbles against her tongue. Loath to deprive herself of a single inch, she dragged her tongue from sac to tip. Jewel delighted in the sharp hiss it brought forth, and the tight, almost desperate grip of his hands in her hair.

She sensed his release loomed near, but he refused to succumb. He drew her head back and looked down at her, his eyes twin flames of black fire. "Oh, no you don't." And he jerked her up so that her breasts slammed against his torso, her already hard nipples tingling with renewed fire.

In that instant, she knew what would come. She knew that look well, the one that said she'd driven him into the too deep, primal level of sex. Her loins combusted with the mere thought of him entering her from behind.

"Turn over." He roared it out, flipping her so that she lay stomach-down across the boulder. Vince pressed his hand into her back, holding her down. She felt him shift and soon discovered what the movement would produce. Roughly, he leaned over her and snatched her hands, bringing them together in front of her on the rock's surface. And with savage precision, he wound and tied the bola's husk-rope around her wrists. As if to further drive his point home, he tossed aside the stones that were still tied to the three ends of the bola cords. They tumbled down the opposite side of the boulder. The jolt of them against her wrists when they plunged out of sight and came to a sudden halt tore a gasp of pain from her throat. But the pain didn't last long. Just being held in this primitive mating position, out under a blazing sun in the wild tropics, was enough to make her come. Her breath caught in her lungs. She fought to breathe against the waves of desire that slammed through her, engorging her pussy, soaking it into a slick canal in preparation for his beastly entry.

He fell on top of her, his wide chest pressed to her back. "Suck it." The command came gruff and forceful in her ear. At first she wasn't sure what he meant. But then she saw the banana he held in front of her face, and carnal joy exploded in her brain. Even with the peel still on, she could smell its sweet scent, could almost taste it in her mouth. Still famished, she obeyed eagerly, her mouth rooting for the non-stemmed end.

At the very moment he shoved the fruit into her mouth, his cock tore into her from behind. She moaned, her teeth biting through the peel. Banana flavor burst in her mouth, and she sucked as if she performed a blowjob on another man while being fucked. His massive shaft speared her like a savage native, filling her with shattering, white-hot sensations deep inside her core. Though her toes barely touched the ground, her entire front side pressed into the warm, hard rock. Her nipples abraded over the rough surface, sending sparks of heat out through her arms, intensifying the pleasant pain of the rope against her wrists. With each thrust he took, bliss loomed nearer, taunting her as her clit throbbed with anticipation. She bobbed on the banana, easily deep-throating it when he forced it in and out between her lips.

"Open your mouth wide," he demanded.

She parted her lips with a tinge of regret, for with it, came the withdrawal of both the tasty fruit and his cock.

"What...? No, please. Don't stop." Her voice sounded husky and submissive to her own ears. She struggled against the binding, trying desperately to see behind her.

"Shh," he coaxed, smacking her ass.

She cried out, her head snapping back. Sharp pain shot through her right ass cheek. Blood rushed to her buttocks, easing the pain with a pleasant tingling sensation that crept around to flood her pussy. The shock of it rendered her speechless. Her mind clouded with an animalistic craving to feel it again, to be overpowered by total male dominance.

He'd never spanked her before, but now that she had a taste of its pleasurable pain, she wasn't letting him get away with just one. "More...please."

"You like that, huh?" She shivered at the raspy, lust-filled tone to his voice, as if he too, were on the edge of insanity.

"I...yes," she whimpered, turning her head to capture his mouth with hers. He indulged her for several delicious moments, his tongue raking her mouth, scraping over her teeth. She tasted fruit and sweat, a potent combination. "I...it feels wicked, almost forbidden."

He moaned at her response. She too couldn't believe the words that poured from her mouth. They seemed to inject them both with a baser hormone. He pushed up from the rock and fumbled nearby, snatching up another banana.

Just when she thought there would be no more torture, he shoved the long, curved fruit into her pussy. The very edges of orgasm reached out to slap her yet receded before she could embrace it. At the very same moment, his hand came down on her left ass cheek, hard and sharp. The smack echoed through the trees, and she thought she heard the surf halt, the birds quiet. It seemed fireworks burst in her head, fluttered across her vision. She pushed against his thrusts, her toes digging into the hot sand. The thick banana slid in and out of her, even as he swatted her, his big, hot palm making repeated, firm contact with her soft ass. Clenching her teeth with a growl, she pistoned her pussy into his forceful rhythm, grinding her clit into the rock.

"Oh... Oh...I'm going to—" He cut her off by ripping the fruit from inside her. She looked up just in time to see the banana hurled over her head, straight across the clearing. It tumbled into a low palmetto, cradled almost perfectly within its long leaves.

Frustration set in. Her skin crawled with a desperate need for carnal release. She couldn't move, couldn't turn, couldn't even reach her hand down to her throbbing clit to finish herself off. Hot elixir oozed from her canal.

"Vince." She swallowed, her mouth now parched from all the excessive panting. "Please. Take me now. Make me come. Give me your cock before I go crazy. *Now!*"

She didn't have to wait long. On a gasp, she braced for his entry. He tore into her, burying himself so deeply, she could feel his tight balls press against the lips of her cunt. He gripped the ropes of the restraint in one hand and wound, easing the weight of the rocks on her wrists. By doing so, he was able to lift her hips, just enough to slide his other hand in between her and the rock. With targeted accuracy, he located her nub. She cried out in pure gratitude when he rubbed the tip of his finger frantically, expertly over its hardness. Simultaneously, he rocked his body fast and furiously against her ass. Her muscles clamped down on his length, holding desperately, impatient for bliss to overtake her.

"Oh God," she screamed. "Here I come! Oh, don't stop, Vince, please, please. Ah...*oh!*" Her eyelids fluttered shut and she saw neon flashes. The orgasm washed through her with breathtaking beauty and color. The flavors of the fruits she'd gorged on, orange, banana, his cum, all burst in her mouth. Her hot, sticky syrup coated Vince's dick, and the aroma of it rose into the humid air around them. She jolted, struggling to rise up on her elbows even as the rope held her hands captive. With one last glorious wave, she sighed out her gratitude.

He suddenly withdrew, and she felt him stiffen and suck in a ragged breath. She started to turn, to see why he delayed his own pleasure, but he knocked the air from her as he fell on top of her once again. She clamped her eyes shut, preparing for another delicious assault.

On one long groan, he shoved his cock into her, his body shuddering with release. She rejoiced, complete love filling her heart.

But her eyelids flew open when he sighed out, "Jewel. Ah...I finally got my jewel back."

Chapter Seven

She fought against him like a wildcat. The sudden wiggling and kicking, along with her strangled cry, had him jumping back with a jolt of confusion. To have his cock go from the tight slickness of her, to hot, humid air in a matter of milliseconds, was painful, to say the least. The backside of her bare, glossy body, her slit engorged and sticky, flailed against the weight of the bola restraint on her arms.

Finally, she rolled off the rock, and with a thud, she landed on her ass in the sandy soil. Her eyes glowered up at him with fury like he'd never seen before. Something about the combination of that primitive emotion, coupled with her current state of sex-tousled disarray and physical restraint, punched him right in the gut with overwhelming affection.

"You son of a bitch."

He noted her voice remained husky, but it was slowly healing, and he could detect the old Jewel deep in its tone. Vince crossed his arms over his chest, slid a look down at her. "Now, is that any way to treat the man who just took you to euphoria and back?"

"Oh!" She jerked her arms against the ropes that were still attached to the heavy rocks. "You tricked me."

"Tricked you? How so?"

"You just called me Jewel."

He went dizzy for the briefest moment. Had he really blown his cover — or hers, rather? Shit. He'd hoped to keep that advantage over her until he could figure out just why she'd chosen to deceive him. Besides, he thought with an inward chuckle, he'd been thoroughly enjoying having that secret tidbit of knowledge. But too late now. Obviously in the archaic, animal state of mind she'd had him in, he'd let his lion out of the damn bag.

"And that means *I* tricked *you*?"

"You knew all along." Her eyes narrowed. She got to her feet with all the grace a woman could while tied to a bola, naked and angry as a snarling cat.

He watched as she hunched, leaning down to frantically work her wrists from the ropes. "And you didn't?"

"Of course I know who I am! But you obviously knew as soon as you laid eyes on me again," she accused.

"Uh-uh. Only after I saw the tattoo on your beautiful ass — and the mole at the nape of your neck. *And*," he added, feeling his own anger spike, "the six earring holes in the cartilage of your left ear that, for some reason, you seemed to no longer be using."

Her eyes went wide with shock, and he took great satisfaction when that look slid into frustration.

"Forgot about my name being etched right onto your gorgeous ass, Jewel?" He didn't wait for her to reply. "Well, I've never forgotten it. And I recognized it right away when you turned your much slimmer back on me in the bungalow. You promptly — without a fucking worry in hell, by the way — fell into a contented sleep after shaking my world with your passion. There you lay, different body, different face and hair, different voice. But the same brand is still on your ass, the same mole's still there, and the very same fiery, eager sex-kitten I used to know so well, still lurks beneath the surface. Only more so."

"So, tell me..." Vince strode forward, unable to stand watching her continued struggles. He knelt and untied the cords, freeing her. "Am I really to conclude that you conveniently were stricken with amnesia?"

She rubbed her wrists and jerked her loincloth down into its proper place. "Of course I knew who I was, you idiot." Locating her halter-top, she snatched it up and tied it into place, caging those luscious breasts in and away from his prying stare.

He got to his feet. "But you didn't tell me—and it's not like it was an easy puzzle to solve, at least not at first. You've been hiding it from me ever since we got here. And *that's* trickery if I've ever seen it."

Her fists jammed onto her curvy hips. The wind blew in, ruffling her golden locks around her ire-reddened face. She spoke through her teeth. "It's called protecting myself. Now go away. Just go far, far away, damn you."

Spinning on her heels, she marched to the tree house. Her hourglass shape taunted him as her rear wiggled with each step she took.

"Um, babe, you've got sand all over your ass and thighs," he said as he followed her. "And I'd guess there's some stuck to your...privates, given the fact that area was soaking wet, and you fell into the sand shortly after..."

"Tell me about it," she snarled over her shoulder, shuffling carefully, as if the grains even now irritated her pussy. She swatted sand from the backs of her thighs as she moved away from him. "And how many times do I have to tell you not to call me babe?"

He ignored her question and threw out another. "Want a bath?"

"A bath?" She stopped and turned, unable to hide the longing in her eyes, exactly what he guessed would happen. "Yes. Yes, I do. Do you know…is there a water hole, a bathing place of some sort?"

"Haven't found one of those yet."

Her shoulders sagged. She glared at him, as if to nonverbally label him as a vile and hateful creature for taunting her with mere mention of a bath. With a huff, she spun, heading for the ladder. He followed.

"Hold on, spitfire. There's a path just past the tree house there. It'll lead you a short distance to the opposite end of the island from the one we landed on. Go take a dip in the Gulf and rinse off before you get some of those grains up inside your—"

He nearly bumped into her when she whirled on him. The scent of pussy and oranges wafted up to tease his nostrils. Golden shafts of sunlight bathed her creamy skin. He longed to run his hands over its silky texture again, its color just starting to take on a light tan hue from all the spotty sun exposure during their trek.

Her eyes snapped fury and humiliation. "Vince. Shut up. Just shut up."

Holding up his hands, he backed away. "Shutting."

He stared up at her, watching intently as she scaled the ladder. The twin swells of that ass peeped out at him as she climbed. She disappeared, but reemerged with some of the contents from the chest. Clutching shampoo, soap, toothpaste and a toothbrush lovingly in her arms, she strode up to him.

"I'd really like to know…how did you learn to do all this?" The hand holding the shampoo bottle swept the campground. "And this?" She pointed her foot outward to indicate her bandaged ankle.

"I learned it a long time ago, long before I even met you. It's not really that important. "

Sadness washed over her face. His heart lurched. "You never made any indication that this—this…Tarzan guy hid beneath that conceited, carefree exterior. It seems you've duped me, as well. You've been a fake all along."

Her accusation hit him square in the gut of his male ego. He seriously thought about walking away, but that's what she'd done. It was the coward's way out of turmoil and tension. No, Vince Santiago never turned his back on a challenge, whether it was to see to survival needs, or to finally put a woman in her place, if need be.

"I was in the military, Jewel. Special Operations. I was made to learn things that've been ingrained in me permanently, whether I want to forget them or not. When suddenly thrown back into an environment that warranted survival, my skills kicked in again. Just like riding a bicycle. But I hardly saw a need to brag to you about something that I don't view as a talent required to be put on a relationship résumé. Just as I didn't inform you that I can not only ride that bicycle, but parachute, pilot a chopper, fire an M-16 with excellent marksmanship and kill the enemy in cold blood. Then I can turn right around and butcher innocent little game, and wolf it down with eager, hungry finesse."

Her face turned a lovely shade of green. "That's enough, Santiago."

"What's the matter?" He stepped close enough that he could almost hear her heart thud in her chest. "Scared? Perplexed? Feeling a bit betrayed?"

"No."

"Bullshit."

"Yes."

"Well, then," he ground out, his temper pricked, "now you know how I felt when you marched out of my life."

She lifted her chin and spun, leaving behind a cloud that mingled with his own scent upon her skin. "I'm done with you, Vince. I'm going to go take a bath."

"Yeah, done with me. That's what you said four years ago. But, Jewel?" He snatched her elbow just before she sailed out of reach. She winced, looking up at him with a murderous sparkle in her eyes.

"What?"

"It's all too obvious. I'm not done with you yet, and you're not done with me."

She jerked free of his hold and stomped away. He watched as she followed the path he'd cleared. Gradually, she disappeared around a bend.

But he was going after her.

He glanced up at the spotty patch of dark clouds moving in. Wind suddenly whipped up, making the flames beneath the roasting wild boar dance and sputter. Oh yes. Once he got everything gathered up and tucked safely into the tree house against the coming storm, he would go after her. He would find out once and for all what she'd done to herself, why her looks had changed so drastically, why he hadn't been able to, at first, see who she was through the new mask.

And he would find out why she left him four years ago without an explanation, without a goddamn word since.

Vince doused the flames with sand, and smoke curled up to lick the meat. He lifted the fully cooked pig and set it upon several spread cocoyam leaves. Leaving it to cool, he took some of the water he'd sterilized from the plantain tree trunk and placed it inside their shelter for future use. While there, he restrung Jewel's hammock and secured all the windows with their drop panels of bamboo-covered matting. Next, he made certain the fedegoso leaves he'd used to prepare the salve for her ankle, remained plentiful and at the ready.

A shiver of worry shot up his spine. Thank God he'd found that fedegoso tree. Just speculating what could have occurred if he hadn't, churned his stomach and broke him out in a trembling sweat.

Shaking off the morbid thought, he went down and wrapped the pig in the cocoyam leaves. He hauled it up and placed it inside the shelter before returning to the site to collect as many coconuts as he could, including the few he'd let dry in the sun. Those, too, he'd include in their stock, for there was no way to tell how long they'd be holed up in the coming storm.

Living quarters now readied, he went down to gather up all the edible vegetation he'd collected. As he loaded his arms with oranges, he spotted the banana he'd fucked her with. Crossing to the palmetto bush where it had landed after he'd thrown it in a sexual frenzy, he plucked the fruit up, closed his eyes and ran it under his nose. Her juices were dried upon the smooth, slightly bruised yellow skin, but he could still detect her musky-sweet fragrance anywhere. He stuck out his tongue, ignoring the violent gusts of wind around him. And he just couldn't resist. He licked her flavor from the surface.

"Ah, Jewel...I just want to eat you alive." His voice carried on the wind. "I just can't get enough of you."

Taking the fruit between his lips, he sank it deep into his mouth, his tongue swirling around the candy-coated banana. Hunger and a wild, sudden need for her washed through him as her sweet spice burst on his taste buds.

He groaned around the bulk in his mouth. Heavy heat sank into his loins and he felt his dick begin to harden. Freeing his half-hard cock from the tattered garment, Vince clutched it in one hand, moving the banana in and out of his mouth with the other. He just couldn't help himself. Need assailed him, undeniable. Like a wild wolf tracking his mate in heat, he devoured the remnants of her. And he suddenly knew there was no other way but to relieve himself during her absence. Her scent, her taste, her nearby presence, all drove him to have her again. But now that her anger had come back full force, he was most certain he'd have a fight on his hands if he went to seek her out for his release.

So he'd have her anyway...in his mind.

* * * * *

Jewel had gotten to the beach when she realized she'd forgotten to bring a piece of the scrap blanket to use as a towel. Leaving the toiletries behind, she'd trotted up the path, racing to beat the coming storm. Arriving back into the camp, she squinted, bringing Vince into focus where he stood under a palm tree, very close to the exact spot where he'd just ravished her. As she neared, she almost gasped aloud when she heard him speak of eating her alive. His words, said without the knowledge of her being there, stunned her to breathlessness. She inhaled, her head spinning into an erotic whirlwind. Her heart palpitated, her throat went dry and her pussy throbbed with a sudden vengeance. Winds gusted around them, and his hair fluttered, the musky scent of him mixed with her own aroma filled her lungs.

She watched his massive profile, standing just behind and to his right, positioned in order to see what he did in detail, but remain undetected at the same time. Spellbound, she stared in disbelief while he deep-throated the very banana he'd shoved up inside her. The long, fluid muscles in his back and side flexed and glistened in the waning light with each movement he made. She nearly whimpered aloud when his free hand released his cock, already half erect, apparently just from tasting her on the fruit. Something about it made her grind her teeth with beastly aggression. She struggled to calm her rapid breathing, to remain quiet, to not reveal herself, to not disturb him in this irresistible, unexpected show. Honey dribbled out between her legs. Unable to refrain, she reached down and slid her hand into the front of her skirt.

As Vince tasted her and jacked off, she found her moist bud and swirled her finger around it. Her eyes devoured him. She licked her lips, longing to taste him as he tasted her. The free hand that had been trembling at her side fluttered up her belly and cupped her breast, pinching the already taut nipple between her fingers. Fire jolted through her with each flicker of her finger on her clit, each tweak of her areola, each movement of his hand upon his thickening rod. She heard him groan, and his rhythm quickened, long, strokes of pure male practiced precision.

Jewel knew it would be a quick one for them both. But she also knew she must come first so that she could fade back into the forest without being noticed before he reached his own pinnacle. Frantic, she spread her legs in a stance and bore her gaze into him. His eyes were closed and he had his head thrown back while he rubbed himself, the banana still pumping in and out of his mouth. She released her nipple and shoved her hand down to join the other. With one finger taking her on a lusty ride across her clit, she sank another into her wet pussy. It was just what she needed. Her vision blurred with the oncoming orgasm. It shook her with a torrential force, spattering her at the very moment she heard him groan out her name. White fluid spurted from the tip of his penis.

Fighting her own pleasure and her body's natural responses, she stiffened when a cry escaped from deep within her throat. A second, unexpected orgasm gripped her so tight, she was unable to release herself. But even as the last ripples warmed her, humiliation froze in her soul. He whipped his head around spotting her standing there with both arms plunged into her skirt like a shameless slut.

Mortified, she let out a strangled cry and ripped her hands out of her garment. "Oh my God—no!" She twirled with a stumble and ran as fast as she could on the path toward the sea. Jewel raced to a cool bath to cleanse herself of this hot, relentless sex drive that had forced her to watch the man she loved give a banana a blowjob while he played with himself.

No, please no. He couldn't know just how much it had turned her on. *But he did know, Jewel.* Greedy, unable to resist that second crest, she'd blown her cover, and now she would be forced to face him again after he'd seen her with her hands down her skirt. Watching him. Coming. Just like a jungle beast.

But she refused to think that she'd been doing the very same uncivilized things he'd been doing.

Lurching into the dense brush, she batted aside hanging moss and low-lying limbs. Her feet carried her speedily, regardless of the sharp shells that bit at her arches. The pound of the surf grew closer. Bursting onto the beach, she dove into the choppy waves, heedless of the distant rumble of thunder and streaks of lightning barreling in from the horizon.

* * * * *

Vince swore biting out words even a hardened pirate would balk at. It wasn't the fact that she'd seen him that had him lashing out at himself. It was his lack of self-control. Sure, he'd obviously turned her on enough to make her engage in a bit of voyeurism while masturbating—and oh, how *that* sexy sight wouldn't be soon forgotten. But the new turmoil and tension the whole event would undoubtedly cause between them were his own fault. If only he'd been able to resist his damn juvenile urges, he thought with disgust as he raced after her.

"Christ, you're a brainless animal, Santiago," he sneered out loud.

He emerged from the halophytes onto the beach just in time to see her rise from the sea to the shallow edge where her toiletries lay. Water sluiced down over her clothed body as she squirted shampoo onto her palm and hurriedly lathered her hair. By leaving on her clothes, she'd protected her flesh from his prying eyes—or so she thought. More so than if she'd been naked, he could make out every detail of her beneath the thin, soaked fabric. Just knowing she'd been carelessly naïve made him want to trudge in after her, snatch her up and carry her to bed.

Instead, he studied her ritual, inhaled the scent of soap when she plucked it up and sudsed it between her hands. She scrubbed her face, her arms and shoulders, and slid a hand into her top. Her lashes fluttered, her mouth rounded out with a sigh as she cleansed the sensitive peaks. Thunder cracked in the distance and her eyes flew open. Jewel re-lathered her hands and jerked up her skirt. Quickly, and with one too many gasps, she bathed her pussy, sliding her fingers between the lips, brushing over the clitoral area.

In total disbelief, Vince realized his cock grew hard once again. It had been years since he'd had so many orgasms, so many erections in such a short time. He marveled at it, and wondered if it had anything to do with Jennie or Luke's hocus-pocus, and the fact he'd been stranded on their *Carnal* Island.

He studied her as those long legs became frothed in bubbles. She turned slightly away and bent to stroke her calves. Wind roared in and flapped her skirt over the small of her back. The waves—much more volatile now that the sun had been concealed behind a curtain of ominous clouds—crashed around her ankles and feet. The move presented him with a front-on view of her luscious ass and slit. His balls ached with renewed longing. What he wouldn't do to sink himself between those ass cheeks.

"Get a grip, asshole," he mumbled, watching as she tossed aside the bar of soap and dove into the arc of a wave. She reemerged five yards out and ducked her head several times to rinse her hair.

Slowly, she trudged against the turmoil of water and wind, materializing from the bath, bringing to mind that sultry sea nymph once again. He could see every curve and plane of her ripe, wet body. His hands flexed, yearning to cup those full breasts, to take that plump mouth with his.

With careful control, he stepped forward until he saw her eyes snap with awareness. She inhaled closing her lids briefly, as if to rein in her ire at his interruption—or was it to hide in shame? Movements jerky, she bent to pluck up the assortment of cleansing items.

"Go away, Vince." Fat rain droplets began to spatter upon the choppy water's surface. Lightning streaked overhead followed by an angry rumble of thunder. While the air cooled, it danced with electricity and energy, much as Jewel did. "Please, just go away."

"There's a storm coming."

"Really?" The single word came out sharp and sarcastic. She sidestepped him and headed for the path.

"We need to get back to the shelter before—"

Jewel screeched, cutting off his words. He braced himself against the flash of lightning, flicked his gaze over when it struck a nearby palm. It sparked and smoked. The abrupt yet drawn-out sound of cracking wood followed. And the tree toppled in slow motion, blocking their path back to camp. A five-foot wave rolled in, crashed upon the packed sand. Another followed, bigger still. The scent of a cool, angry rain blew in, and with it, the curtain of raindrops moved closer. It swept them with livid speed, spikes of wetness spattering upon warm flesh.

"Before one of us gets hurt," he continued.

She ducked her head, clutching the items to her chest. He caught the look of embarrassment, as if an image of what she'd just done while watching him, suddenly flitted through her mind. The rosy hue of her cheeks, combined with the humiliation in her eyes, somehow served to further inflame him, even with the threat of danger moving in around them.

"Please, please, just don't look at me." She choked it out and sprinted across the beach. Still holding the soaps, she sat on the fallen tree, swiveled her legs over to the other side and took off into the woods.

Ducking at the crack and rumble above him, he followed behind her. Within minutes, he entered the camp just in time to see her scurry up the ladder.

But now she was trapped in his lair. The time had finally come to interrogate his witness. And he wasn't about to let her plead to the fifth.

* * * * *

"You do have another choice, Jensina," Justina told her.

Fraught with worry over her failing mission, Jennie had dragged Luke into the Xanthian realm to consult with her sister, the queen. Their plan, while having its promising moments, seemed to veer off and crash into a wall at every turn. And mostly because of that stubborn woman, Jewel Dublin.

"Sister, I would greatly appreciate any suggestions you may have." Jennie wrung her hands together. With her dark hair in a twist of silk at the crown of her head, the silver streaks she'd earned during her graduation process to Goddess now framed her delicate face. Luke ground his teeth, resentment filling his soul at the agony marring those lovely features.

"Between Jewel's obstinacy," she went on, her voice tight, "and Vince's ability to suddenly scare her off like an ogre, I fear our mission will go awry. And I fear — "

"I'm telling you, Justina. You put her back in that damn bottle," Luke couldn't help interrupting with a growl, "you might as well put me in there with her, or else..." He paced back and forth across the veranda of the queen's castle, unable to ignore the scents of hibiscus and roses as they wafted up from the garden. Beyond the patio, the maze of plant life spread far and wide, a glorious splash of color against the lavender and pale green streaks of the Xanthian sky. Rich with every species of trees, shrubs, flowers and plants that existed in the universe, along with some experimental cross-gene varieties, it was a true phenomenon.

"Luke!" Jennie scolded him through clenched teeth, her face now flushed with embarrassment.

"It is all right, Jensina." The queen crossed the chamber with her usual regal air, to her throne set upon a wide marble stage. Luke knew it was the very spot where Queen Justina had performed his mortality-altering operation. He shivered at the thought of his bloody, near-dead heart being ripped from his very chest. But he'd received a new, transplanted, immortal one. A concept he still struggled to get used to.

Justina sat and fanned her shimmering blue gown out around her. Her hair had been twined up much like Jennie's, but she wore a heavily jeweled headdress that left no doubt which one of the two identical twin sisters ruled the entire realm.

"Your Luke is very much the protective alpha. I understand this, and I rejoice in his love for you. However, he must realize," she said with a withering stare that told him who possessed the true magical powers, "that he cannot threaten his queen."

Luke swore silently, his blood pressure rising until his head pounded with fury. Struggling to give his new queen the respect she deserved, and to at the same time make himself very clear, he replied thickly, "And your rules for this love affair to commence in commitment is entirely too strict. We are now in the second day, moving into the third—hardly enough time to patch up these huge rifts that remain between Jewel and Vince. Jennie should not be made to pay in that damn bottle for eternity just for her first failed mission. It's wrong—with all due respect, your highness." He bowed, just to soften the rage that threatened to spill from his soul. "And she should be allowed some practice runs, if you ask me."

Justina steepled her fingers, peering at him cryptically over their tips. She rested her delicate elbows on the gold-encrusted arms of her throne. "What I'll ask you, and please, correct me if I'm wrong, is... Did you not choose the subjects yourself, Luke Slayton, my God of Carnality?"

"Yes, but—"

"Luke, she is right. Now, please," Jennie begged, stomping one foot. "Just hold your tongue and let her speak!"

Justina merely chuckled a melodious sound of approval.

"I will *not* keep my mouth shut and watch you slip from my fingers again. No magic will prevent it." And he folded his arms, just to further emphasize his determination.

Jennie shot him a look of horror tinged with love. She crossed to him, her hands fisted at her sides. When she neared, he caught the ever-alluring fragrance that was only that of Jensina Sebastian Slayton. In the entire universe, there could be no other being that smelled as delicious as his wife.

"You cannot talk to her that way," she said in a low voice.

"I will talk to *anyone* that way who threatens you with another banishment. This time, it's to be a permanent one. I tell you, it's not happening as long as I live." He shifted his stance and chuckled hollowly. "And last time I checked, that queen over there made me immortal, which means I'm not dying anytime soon."

Jennie sighed and closed her eyes. He could see the pulse thumping in her throat, and he longed to kiss that very spot to still her nerves.

"Queen," she began, spinning to face her sister. "I beg your forgiveness for my husband's arrogance and disrespect."

"I can beg my own forgiveness, babe," he snarled.

"Now, now." Justina soaked them both with a slightly scornful look, as if to scold two quarreling children. But it seemed her inborn sense of humor was her best asset as the ruler of a vast realm. She smiled, slow and warm. "Let's put away the emotions, my two lovebirds, and get back to the important matter at hand. I forgive your Luke—at least *this* time. Now, as I was trying to say moments ago, you do have another alternative, Jensina."

Jennie pressed her hand into her belly. "I'm not so sure I want to hear this."

She frowned almost mockingly. "Well, all right then. You're both dismissed. Complete your mission by the end of the third day or dear sister, face imprisonment."

"No, wait!" Jennie and Luke breathed in unison.

She smiled with a knowing nod. "That's precisely what I thought."

"Please." Jennie glided across the chamber and knelt before her sister. She hung her head, suspending her hand out at her side as a sign to Luke to join her in subservience. He sighed and went to her, bowing before the queen.

"I beg of you..." Jennie went on. "Please educate me on my alternative, my almighty queen."

"Rise, sister, brother-in-law." She clapped two sharp notes of demand. Her voice rang strong with an edge of harshness. "No need for formalities among family."

Jennie rose slowly and Luke followed. He grappled with the urge to wrap his hands around the creamy golden column of Justina's neck and squeeze the immortal life from her.

"You may abort the mission if you so choose. While the very nature of the type of magic used to implement the action cannot be negated from your protégés' minds, you still have time to back out and begin anew with different subjects."

"You mean once they are transported back to their places of origination, they will still remember their experiences on Carnal Island?"

She nodded. "It can be a risk for them. The seemingly bizarre experience, particularly for Jewel, could be life-altering to the point of mental devastation. Now, I'll tell you it seems you've misunderstood…you've been granted a free trial run, in a sense, not just one do-or-die opportunity. So, if you don't abort and don't fulfill the plan, you still have another chance beyond this one." She breezed past and glided to the archway, looking out over her land. Her voice, so like Jennie's, held that extra quality of imperialness that Jennie's did not. No, his passionate wife's voice had an added sultry note to it not found in Justina's.

"But," Justina went on, "if before the end of the third day, they should come together anyway—even if you've aborted—per the rules and regulations, you will still be rewarded. But you will only receive *half*-credit."

"Let me get this straight." Luke just couldn't remain silent anymore. He longed to get this in writing, but chose to accept verbal confirmation. "Removing them from Carnal Island will erase the constraints of the three-day, crucial timeframe, but not their memory of their experiences. However, the clock will still tick on the spell. Once they're back home, if they should still come together by the end of those initial three days, Jennie will still get credit—in spite of aborting—yet there won't be the threat of being banished?"

"Correct, but she will only receive a half-credit. Which will require an extra mission, beyond Vince and Jewel's, to make this one count as a whole, complete, victorious one."

"And how many missions does Jennie have to conclude victoriously before she no longer has to worry about the two-strikes-and-she's-out stipulation?"

"Well…" Justina bit her lower lip. Her long soot eyelashes fluttered. "She only need complete one *full* and successful mission to be finally left alone without fear of ever being banished to eternity. That means she really only gets one 'strike,' as you call it, of failure before meeting with success on the second try. Now, if she should abort, then gain half-credit if Vince and Jewel should unite before the end of three days, then she's in a sense caused herself to require *two* successful half missions instead of one whole non-aborted one. If she conquers her second mission, the one following the half-credit one, that is, she need not ever worry about the 'strikes' again. You see, one-half plus one-half always equals one, even here in Xanthus." She grinned almost playfully.

"So my choices are," Jennie asked, her eyes now sparkling with hope and relief, "to take the chance of uniting them before the three days are up...*or* abort before that and hope they unite anyway. Which will afford me a half-credit. Which will, in turn, cause me to have to endure an extra mission and another half-credit, in order to be out of danger of banishment forever."

"An extra *successful* mission," Justina corrected. "But, yes. You have the essential law of it correct, in summary."

Jennie merely heaved a sigh. And Luke silently seconded that. It was really a quite confusing technicality, if you asked him.

"Should Jennie call a halt to this task, can we still use our influences, even though we're not within the boundaries of the island?"

"Yes, but not *genie* influences. Magical persuasion of any sort will not be allowed. Once you've chosen to negate the three-day spell ahead of time and return them to the very spots where you abducted them from, magic will be prohibited as a tool of influence. You can visit, you can talk and persuade *verbally* only, but that is the limit of it. The only supernatural forces you may use are for your own movement from place to place, and use of the Xanthian Big Screen. No spells, no magic."

"So, either we continue on Carnal Island, let the clock run out with access to full genieatic powers and hope for the best before it does run out... *Or* we negate the initial spell and hope for unity anyway, with a half-point loss—or gain, however you choose to look at it—and no strikeout."

"Precisely."

"Must we choose now?" Jennie's voice held a tone of indecision and anxiety.

Justina shook her head, rising. She looked down at Jennie. "Technically, you have until the final minute of the spell to decide. But not one millisecond longer."

Chapter Eight

"Where have you been all these years?" Vince laced his fingers behind his head and stared up at the thatched ceiling. One leg slung over the edge of the hammock, he pushed himself with a foot, swinging lazily.

Outside, the winds howled, the outer walls pounded by violent rainfall. Flashes of lightning and deafening thunder raged on beyond their protective shelter. He'd found some candles and matches buried in the trunk, and the room now flickered with dancing shadows upon the walls. The air wasn't musty at all like he'd expected it to be. The genies had obviously provided them with cool, pleasant temperatures.

Temperatures conducive to lovemaking...

The faint fishy scent of the tossed sea and wild vegetation permeated the closed room, masked only by that of the still-warm roast pig. Briefly, he wondered if a hurricane could be in the forecast. But somehow, he knew instinctively these four walls would withstand anything, as long as he and Jewel were inside working on their relationship. He'd come to the conclusion that this entire adventure had been devised as nothing more than a matchmaking reunion on Luke and Jennie's part.

And he no longer had any reservations about that particular plan.

But Jewel did. He slid his gaze over and watched as she huddled on the floor in a corner and tore off a strip of ham with her teeth. She chomped and smacked ravenously, and it brought to mind an uncivilized, beautiful tribal woman reduced to the baser needs. She'd slept for what he'd estimated to be nearly eighteen hours during the course of her infection. Since waking, he mused, hunger and thirst of various sorts had overtaken her.

He thought now as he watched her below lowered lids that she looked like Tarzan's Jane might, if there were really such characters. Vince remembered a much prissier Jewel than the one he saw now. And the hunger that drove her to devour the meat with such zest, made him all the more determined to assist the genies in completing their little plan. They would get back to civilization soon, he vowed. She would never again be reduced to a heathen state of existence, not if he could help it.

"Um, hello?"

Jewel's head snapped up. Her mouth and chin glistened with grease. She spoke around her food. "Hmm? What?"

"I said where have you been all these years?"

"Oh." She swallowed, swiped the back of her hand across her mouth. "Vermont. Teaching."

"Vermont? Why'd you choose to move from Denver to such an out-of-the-way state as Vermont?"

Jewel plucked up a banana and peeled it with quick precision. Just watching her hold the fruit in her hand brought to mind her cream-soaked pussy. A vague, underlying tingle of desire swept through him. But first things first, he thought.

She bit off a large hunk and chewed, her eyes watching him with guarded interest. "To get as far away from you as I could, why else?" Her sharp words sliced precise and to the quick. But he'd recently come to the conclusion they were merely a defense against the strong feelings she had for him. Feelings she wasn't quite sure what to do with. And that delighted him to no end.

"Ah, I see." He flexed his hands behind his head, causing his biceps to tighten. Just as he'd planned, her gaze wondered to his arms, his naked chest.

She tore her stare from him and yanked the peel down further. "Teaching the children in the convent school is only the beginning. I intend to…to become a…a…"

"You're kidding. A convent?"

Jewel tipped back a coconut shell and drank. "Nope. Not kidding."

"Why? Why not just a regular public school like you taught at in Denver?"

He'd always admired the fact that she was a dedicated teacher with a knack for getting through to the most difficult student. But he could hardly see her using that talent in a strict convent. It seemed already obedient children would not challenge her nearly as much.

"To become familiar…with the setting." She avoided his gaze and suddenly made herself busy with cleanup.

Vince suppressed the urge to rise and go to her, to tip up her grease-splattered chin so that those emerald jewels had no choice but to look him directly in the eye. No. He'd silently vowed he'd wring everything from her tonight, and intimidation, for the moment, would only prove counterproductive.

"Familiar for what reason?" He chuckled hollowly. "To become a nun or something?"

Her head swiveled around lethal-fast. He saw in her eyes a conglomeration of indignation, awkwardness and surprise. They locked stares for a long moment before he spoke.

"No, don't tell me," he groaned with a shake of his head. "You went to Vermont to teach in a convent, because you'd planned to become a nun? Fiery, sex-kitten Jewel Dublin, a nun?" He tried, but he couldn't stifle the laughter that rolled from his throat.

Jewel rose slowly. Her eyes drilled him with hatred. "You are an asshole."

He ducked when she winged the banana peel at him.

"Uh-oh, those kids are in for it. A potty-mouthed, violent nun. Hmm…" He stroked his chin, shaking his head with mock confusion.

The rims of her eyes glittered with tears. "This is precisely why I left you, you jerk."

Ah, now they were getting somewhere. "Because I'm being honest in admitting I can't see you as a nun? I mean, it's not meant as an insult, babe. It's just that, even though you have a big heart, that doesn't mean you're nun material. Don't you know…nuns are celibate?"

"Of course I know that!"

Wary of her temper, he studied her closely as she made herself busy by snatching up dates, mangoes and empty coconut shells. Instead of firing them at him, she shuffled them into a semblance of order, her movements quick and jerky. Despite remaining safe from her wrath, he could have sworn an electric jolt of her anger reached out and slapped him right across the face.

Determined to approach this interrogation productively, he laid back and stretched out again in the hammock. Clasping his hands behind his head, he watched as she struggled to keep her gaze from his near-naked body. "Jewel," he shrugged. "It's noble of you to try, but I'm sorry to say, you're plainly not nun material."

She tore her gaze from him and began to pace in the small confines of the room. Her curvaceous shadow moved across the thatched wall behind her. As she strode back and forth, turning with quick, irritated twitches, her breasts jiggled and bounced. The clean scent of soap and shampoo wafted over to tease him. He watched as her slim, bare feet trekked across the wooden floor. Just seeing them so made him wonder what it would be like to suck those long toes, to lick her arches and massage those strong ankles. The bandage on her wound reminded him of how close she'd come to a possibly deadly infection...and made him very aware of some fierce, protective feelings welling up inside him. Before arriving here, he'd never taken such detailed, emotional note of her. New ways to care for her, to worship and seduce her bombarded him at every turn. Every inch of her body, every nuance of her personality, seemed sharper and more defined than before.

Had he taken her for granted all those years ago? Had their tamer sex life back then been the catalyst that had prompted her to leave him? Just wondering if it could be true bruised his ego. If it were true, she'd flung her insults at him correctly. He'd been a self-centered asshole, just like she'd said only minutes ago.

He inhaled deeply, redirecting his suddenly paranoid mind. *Don't jump to conclusions, Vince. Keep up your line of questioning. Your sex life had been great back then. Not nearly as spicy as it has been since arriving here, but you still knew how to please her. There's got to be more to her leaving you than just the possibility of bland sex.*

"Okay, so you're going to be a nun and—"

"Was," she cut in.

"Was? So you've changed your mind."

She stopped in her tracks and he watched as one lone tear rolled down her cheek. "I could hardly hold my head high and be holy when my body burns for you. Which was precisely why I chose it in the first place, to try and purge you from my system. Only now I see it's...it's..."

Her declarative words, though spoken with contempt, made him want to climb to the rooftop and shout his joy. Instead, he remained calm. "Not possible?"

Jewel plopped down next to the roast and covered her face with her hands. Angry sobs tore from her chest. "Oh Vince, you rat! You've totally ruined my future plans. Now what am I going to do with myself? I might as well just say screw it all and become a hooker!"

He chuckled, even as his heart spilled over with affection for her. And he couldn't hold himself back any longer. He crossed and knelt in front of her. Despite her strangled cries and stiff resistance, he gathered her into his arms and felt the hot tears roll off her cheeks onto his chest.

"You're going to teach, Jewel. It's what you do best. What you were born to do, honey." He stroked her back, closing his eyes when she finally relaxed against him. The forceful sobs died to soft whimpers. He inhaled, taking in the womanly scent of her. His hands moved over her skin, and he marveled at the contrast of its satiny texture against his rougher palms. With a surge of tenderness, he kissed her hair, her forehead, her wet cheeks.

Holding her face between his hands, he studied her, noting the necklace the old crone had given her now nestled in her cleavage, while he still wore the ring on his finger. He glanced up and looked hard and steady into her tormented eyes. "Why, Jewel? Why all the changes? You've cut your hair." He stroked his fingers through the thick golden tresses. The candlelight danced and shimmered on the strands as he combed and petted. It was like raking his fingers through pure silk, he thought, fascinated. "And I don't even know...are you a natural brunette or a true blonde?"

"The dark hair was from a bottle. This is my natural color."

"I like it this way," he decided.

"You do?" The tone of surprise in her voice accompanied a flash of astonishment in her eyes.

He tipped and turned her head, studying her hair and face, caressing her with his eyes. "I do. I love the way it's been kissed by the sun, the way the moon made it shine with a gloss when we traveled through the patchy forest. I love the way the sun's lightly bronzed your skin—and the no-makeup look. I really like it on you," he nodded, finally looking into her eyes. "All that time, all those years ago, you must have been hiding your true beauty from me."

She pressed a hand to the back of his. Her gaze circled his face, searching, hesitant. "You mean it? You're not just saying that to appease me because I cried like a brat?"

He smiled. "Well...you can be a brat at times, but no. I mean it."

"And you can be a creep."

He nodded. "I'm working on it. Now, what else? Hmm...you wear glasses, or did before they broke. I guess I'd forgotten you'd worn glasses."

"I always wore contacts before. I guess—I guess I was a bit self-conscious about wearing glasses in front of you, so I rarely did."

"The color..." He pulled her face to his lips and kissed her eyelids. "The real color of your eyes without the contacts takes my breath away. I don't recall ever getting such a good look at them before coming to Carnal Island."

Vince heard the sharp intake of breath. He knew his words were softening her, but he meant each and every one of them. He drew her back and traced a finger down the bridge of her nose. Her eyelids fluttered.

"I know your voice is hoarse because you choked from almost drowning. But what about the very appealing little hump on your nose? And the scars?" He ran his thumbs down along her hairline and ears, noting the way she flinched. "I don't recall them being there before. And then there's all the weight loss..."

Just as he expected, her eyes flashed and she stiffened again. He'd used as gentle a probing technique as he could, but he sensed the latter observances he'd pointed out would put her on guard.

"No, don't push me away, Jewel. Don't." He shook her gently, continuing to hold her head between his hands, even as she pushed against his chest. "I have a right to know what's going on here. You're the same passionate bed partner, the same spitfire personality, but physically, things don't add up."

"Let go of me." She shoved outward against his inner forearms, narrowing her gaze on him. But he held her in place, forcing her to look into his eyes and reveal the motivation behind her little masquerade.

"I'm not stupid, babe. This isn't just a case of dyeing your hair and losing, oh"—he slid a look down at her luscious body—"about forty to fifty pounds. What happened? Why all the drastic changes? So drastic, that I didn't even recognize you at first."

She pressed her lips together and glared at him, but her struggles died down. "It's none of your goddamn business."

"Ah, taking Him in vain. Yet another example of non-nun material."

She shrieked her indignation, but he went on. "Now, either you tell me exactly where you got these scars, or I throw you out into the storm."

"You wouldn't." No, he wouldn't, but she didn't have to know that.

He hooked his arm around her neck to keep her from fleeing and yanked up the hatch door. Rain blew in on a musty gust and splattered her face as he dragged her closer. The ladder clung to the tree trunk below, drenched by rainwater. The wind suddenly howled fierce and angry, as if by opening the exit door, he'd turned up the volume on Mother Nature. The candles danced in protest to the turbulent air, and the light flickered a soft orange across her stunned face. And at that exact moment, almost as if he'd willed it to happen on cue, lightning struck with a deafening crack nearby. Jewel screeched and broke free of his hold, scrambling out of reach.

He slammed the door shut. The resonating sounds of the storm died to a distant hum. "The truth, or you go find your own shelter. And I mean now."

"You're a cruel bastard, Santiago." Even as she shook from fear, her eyes snapped out their own bolts of lightning, striking him with deadly force. "And I hate you."

"Yes," he agreed, crawling on hands and knees toward her. She cowered in the corner, never taking her eyes from him. "You must have hated me to leave me like that four years ago without a word or a forwarding address or a phone number."

He snapped his fingers in her face. She blinked. "*Poof!* Just like that. Gone. No more Jewel."

"Leave *you*? You made it very clear you didn't want me anymore." Her words came out on an incredulous hiss between clenched teeth.

"I made it very clear I didn't want to get married—at the moment. That does not, in my book, equal not wanting you. Now," he went on, gripping her hands to still her desperate flails. "What the hell happened to your face and your nose?"

She turned her face toward the wall. Her voice came out muffled, but he still caught the thick emotion that threatened to spill over. "After you made it clear *you didn't want me anymore*, I left your apartment in a rush. And in my haste to get as far away from you as I could, I had a wreck—a very bad wreck. It required extensive surgeries of both the reconstructive and life-threatening kind. I was in a coma for the first week. And I almost died twice."

* * * * *

Jewel heard him drag in a ragged breath. She got a sort of a twisted satisfaction from hearing that sound after four long years. It may be confession time, she thought triumphantly, but she would be the one to control things this time, despite his overbearing, macho, man-handling crap. She turned, for she just had to see the guilty look on his face.

"A wreck? Oh my God. It was storming that night, wasn't it?" His eyes flared. He raked a hand through his hair. "And you ended up in the hospital?"

"Yes. And you didn't even bother visiting me."

"Visit you?" His brows arched with feigned surprise. My, but he was quite the actor, she mused. "How in the hell could I visit you if I didn't even know you were in the hospital?"

Her world stopped spinning for a split second. But she put a firm mental hand on it, forcing it back into motion.

"Yeah, right." Jewel couldn't take it any longer. Suddenly fatigued, she pushed herself to a standing position. Crossing to her hammock, she collapsed into its cocoon.

"I'm telling you," he growled, leaping to his feet, panther-like. "I did *not* know you had an accident."

Jewel wasn't believing one word of his lame defense. She crossed her arms and stared up at the beamed ceiling bathed by candlelight. Wind wailed shrilly outside, reminding her where she was. Reminding her the dream had turned back into a nightmare.

"Sure, Vince. And you think I'm going to believe that my roommate—my best friend since grade school—wouldn't have informed you? That is, *if* you'd have bothered to call me at the apartment." She rolled her head to the left and snared him with her gaze. "But you didn't, Vince, because you made it very clear it was over."

"Goddamn it, Jewel, you've got it all wrong. I *did* call, dozens of times that entire week after you walked out on me. I left messages on everything—on fucking voice mail and machines. I even left half a dozen messages with Celeste. She said she'd tell you I called. Toward the end of the week, she finally told me you said you didn't ever want me to call again. I wanted you, Jewel. I swear I did."

"Bullshit! I don't believe you."

He closed the space in two long strides. "No, not bullshit. It's true. And in reality, *you* didn't want *me*."

"No…" She shook her head vehemently. He was there looming above her. The aroma of clean man filled her nostrils, even as she held her breath and fought it. He leaned down, gripping the hammock on either side of her, knuckles whitening with rage. Those luscious lips now curled in a snarl, his face hovered over hers but one breath's space from her mouth. Eyes as thick and hot as molasses scorched her to the core, their sweet, emotional flavor tempting her beyond control.

"Well then, I'll just have to *make* you believe me." His mouth swooped down on hers, crushing the very breath from her. She tasted fruit and meat, fire and ice. He plundered her mouth, nearly choking her with passionate emotions. That familiar curl of lust slid around in her belly, taunting, begging for release. But she couldn't allow it again. She knew for a fact Celeste would never lie to her. Therefore, that left Vince as the deceiver, which wasn't news to her.

Stop this now while you can, Jewel. Now!

She let out a groan of regretted pleasure right before her knees came up. With her fists, she pounded on his sides and ·kicked with all her might. The sudden movements took him by surprise, and he broke the kiss with a loud *smack*, rearing back out of range. In the process, his hands let go of the hammock, setting it into a dangerous, precarious swing. Jewel teetered for a long moment, swinging back and forth in wide sweeps. In a flash, she landed on the hard floor with a *humph*, the wind knocked from her chest. Pain shot through her back and into her neck. Stars swam before her eyes.

"You son of a bitch," she growled, dragging herself up to a crouch position.

His grinned response only infuriated her more. "Sorry about that, babe."

"Oh! I told you to quit calling me babe." She stood, her hands flexing with the urge to slap that arrogant smirk from his handsome face.

The smile faded. He sat on his hammock and leaned back, his arms behind his head in that egotistical, delicious position that irked her. With slow deliberation, he crossed his ankles. "Never."

"Why are you doing this to me, Vince? Why?"

"Come here, Jewel," he commanded, never taking his eyes from her.

"No."

His jaw tensed. "I said, come here."

"And I said no."

"The way I see it is," he replied with a lazy drawl that did little to disguise his anger-tinged control, "you either get your ass over here now, or I come and get you. Face it. Luke and Jennie have seen to it that you have nowhere to run to. Babe."

Oh, she was all too aware of the genies' powers, there was no disputing that now. But that aside, she also knew he'd used the term of endearment again just to taunt her into action, to irritate her. Somehow, though, the deep silk of his voice had managed to make her shiver against her will. As did his threat. But if anybody knew Vince Santiago meant what he said at this moment, it was Jewel Dublin. She was certain he would never hurt her physically. But she also knew if she kept defying him, it could possibly result in more explosive sex. Which would be counterproductive for her if she wanted to end this nightmare and salvage her heart.

Hesitantly, she took one step, then another. He made no indication if her obedience pleased him or not, but kept his eyes locked on hers until she finally stood at his side. Looking down on that savage body of his, her heart did a flip in her chest. Unable to resist, she flickered her gaze downward toward his crotch. Too late, she realized she'd made a terrible tactical error. She could see that his cock stood fully erect beneath his loincloth. It was so erect, in fact, that the very head of it peeped out above the upper edge of the fabric. Swift and heavy need assailed her, soaking her own crotch with an involuntary flood of cream.

Okay, so she could never be a nun, she thought, licking her lips. But that didn't mean she had to go to the other extreme. And with a discipline she prided herself on recouping, she tore her gaze from that unbelievable sight and stared at the wall.

"What's the matter, Jewel?" he taunted, and his hand shot out to clamp about her wrist. "Saying your prayers?"

She gasped and looked down just in time to see the rabid fire of determined passion escape his eyes. With one strong, sudden yank, he had her sprawled across his chest, that long rod pressed into her belly. He clamped one arm around her back, imprisoning her in place. His hand let loose of her wrist and stabbed into the hair at the nape of her neck, holding her head poised above his. Eyes sparkling with evil determination, he raised his knees, wiggling and pushing upward until her legs were forced to spread. They dropped on either side of the hammock, her feet barely brushing the floor.

She fought the fire that ignited between her legs when the movement brought her pussy into direct contact with the peeping head of his cock. The desire stoked in her by glancing at his erection, now smoldered into a full-blown inferno. With her legs spread, her miniskirt had been forced up around her hips. It left her no protection between her sticky lips and his steely tip. He released her head, and with one swift move, he snatched a tie at his hip, bucked up against her, and his loincloth vanished with one practiced sweep.

"No," she panted, pressing against his chest. "Please, no."

"Yes, honey, yes. You know you can't deny what we have." He clutched her shoulders and brought her mouth down to his. In that one smooth move, before she realized the danger of it, he tasted her with a gentle kiss that snatched her breath from her chest. Twisting as he devastated her with the kiss, he maneuvered her so that the tip of his dick slid through her outer slit. She fought the throbbing wave of heat between her legs, sure she would combust at any moment. His tongue tore into her mouth at the very instant his shaft invaded her crux. In one swift stroke, he had her impaled upon his rod. She groaned into his mouth, her tongue suddenly eager to fight with his. The flavor of desire, and a love savored in dreams only, filled her senses swift and sure.

His hands were all over her, tracing her spine with rippling tingles, cupping her ass, pinching and driving her down around his hardness. The slickness of her clit rubbed against him, making her cunt spasm and swallow him deeper. Her hands gripped his wide shoulders, the tight deltoids under smooth skin tempting the flesh of her palms, making her knead and grind. She relaxed her bent arms, allowing her nipples to fall completely into his. Already tight, they burst with a shower of need, a moist swish of skin against skin. Jewel inhaled his hot scent and cupped his whiskered face, now shadowed with a two-day growth of beard. The rough texture prickled against her palms, and a surge of hunger washed through her at the savage, male sensation of it.

He's right, she suddenly thought, stroking him with her pussy. There was no denying what they'd had, at least not now while forced to be together. She knew she couldn't fight it anymore, not with his fullness driving her home to bliss. *Why not savor him while you can?* she asked herself, moaning when he nipped her bottom lip between his teeth. But she already knew the answer. There was no way in hell she could ever resist this man. Ever. Which was why, she told herself as the first vague waves of orgasm licked out to touch her, *you must remain in Vermont over sixteen hundred miles away from him.*

The thought of it tore at her heart with sadness. But Vermont would come later. This was now. Now with his cock fully invading her, now with the skim of a hand, the fire of a kiss. She thrust their inevitable futures aside and embraced the present, clamped her muscles around him in a sticky grip of need. Renewed and fueled for inescapable pleasure, Jewel shoved herself up to a sitting position, her feet now planted firmly on the floor. The change in angles made her cry out when the tip of him rubbed against her g-spot. Unable to stop it, the orgasm slammed into her, quick and concise. Imprisoning him within her straddled stance, she cried out, her voice echoing above the drone of wind and spattering rain. Her eyes squeezed shut, and her toes curled against the rough wood slats. She slapped her hands onto his chest, the silky-hard expanse rising and falling with his ragged breathing. She had no doubt this was only the beginning, a showcase of what would come later. Because already, even as the first release ebbed, the second raged just out of reach.

Outside, the ominous winds picked up, the song of it like a freight train bearing down upon them. Energy crackled in the air, hot and cold, pleasure and pain. Jewel looked down at him, and the expression on his face stilled her pulse. If she didn't know better, she would have described it as an almost-love look. His hands reached up to cup her breasts. In her fantasy-riddled mind, she pretended he held her heart in his hands, stroking and loving her until death do they part.

"Jewel, I..." he rasped, his eyes pools of dark, fluid heat.

She bent and brushed her lips against his, tasting the salt of his skin. "Shh, please, Vince. Don't talk. It's okay. Let's just enjoy it while we can."

He pinched her nipples simultaneously. She sucked in a hot gasp of air. Ripples of lust spun in her belly, and almost obediently, she soaked him with her juices.

Vince groaned, suddenly sitting up. He placed his feet on the floor between hers and stood astride the hammock. Hitching her up, he stepped forward so that he had her pinned against the sturdy bamboo pole, the ropes of the hammock ties abrading her ass. When he looked above her head, his eyes lighting with a gleam of mischief, she glanced up. Looped ropes hung from a beam crossing above the top of a horizontal pole. Still filled by him, he leaned his hips into her, sandwiching her between the wall of his body and the pole. Stretching, he drew one rope down. Excitement moved swift and powerful through her body when she realized his intent. Now that he had her stabilized, he raced his hands up her sides, up past her armpits, until her arms were forced above her head.

"Vince..." She swallowed, feeling his fiery breath fan her breasts. He snaked his tongue out and flickered it over one nipple. "Oh...yes," she rasped on a moan, "just do it, Vince. Tie me up and fuck me. Now."

He blinked. Utter surprise and delight washed over his face. "Oh God, Jewel. I love it when you let go. When you turn into my little nympho."

"I'm going to come. I can feel it now," she panted, devouring his mouth. "As soon as you tie my wrists—oh God!"

Skillfully, as if she were his rodeo prize, he clamped her hands above her head, wound the rope around her wrists and tied it snuggly. He swirled the free end around his hand and tugged until she felt the pulley action of her body being lifted ever so slightly. Tying the other end of the cord off on a lower peg, he now had her strung up against the pole, the ropes of the hammock beneath her ass barely brushing her buttock cheeks. The movement had lifted her a few inches higher so that his cock now only half penetrated her. Her feet no longer touched the ground, but his did. He had all the control, all the leverage and all the domination of a wild beast hungrily eyeing his prey in bondage. His eyes glazed with the knowledge of it. She longed to have him fully inside her again, and struggled against the restraint, fighting for what she craved.

"Fuck me, Vince, all the way. Get it all the way inside me."

He rocked his hips, moving in and out of her so that upon exit, the tip of the head barely remained inside her. Somehow, the withdrawal made her clit throb harder with need. He groaned at the precise moment she did. Her vision blurred as she saw the very boundaries of the coming orgasm. Spurts of her cum frosted his cock with a milky wetness. He buried his face in her breasts, now two submissive melons to feast on at his complete disposal. She screamed her pleasure when he lifted them both, sucking the nipples into his mouth at the same time. God, how she longed to wrap her arms around his head and smother him in her breasts! Flames of wet lust licked at her, burning a trail from her areolas to her womb. And suddenly, Vince shifted his stance and reared up, shoving his cock completely into her canal.

"Yes! Again—again!"

With repeated, quick calf-raises, Vince fucked her while she hung above him. He reached to her very core. The pole pressed long and hard into her back. Against her ass, the hammock ropes rubbed her raw, sending waterfalls of ecstasy into her genitals. Perspiration glistened across both of their bodies, the candlelight lending them a sparkling sheen.

Desperate now, she wrapped her fingers around the tie and pulled herself up in quick jerks so that her cunt pistoned onto his shaft. Teeth clamped tight, she groaned and struggled against the rope, fighting to mate with her

Tarzan. Her legs tightened around him so that she was able to gain more leverage. And with one final lift, she screamed and slammed herself down upon him at the same moment he rose up. Swell after swell of euphoria jolted through her.

He shuddered beneath her, his hot seed shooting into her even as her spasming muscles milked it from him.

Pulse pounding in her throat, wrists raw and on fire, she gasped, "Vince, I...I..." But the words wouldn't come. He looked up at her, a glow of sexy admiration in his eyes. Though she longed to rip her arms down and wrap them around him, to speak her love for him, she somehow knew this would be their last encounter. And she knew voicing her love for him would only make it more difficult to bear a future without him.

He stood there, stroking her skin, pressing soft kisses over her breasts, up her neck, along her jaw line. Goose bumps of contentment shimmied up her spine.

He'll never know the reason you came to him that night to demand a commitment. The thought speared into her brain clear and sure. Her resolve strengthened, as did her love for him.

As if the dire vow possessed the force of a hurricane, the winds outside roared louder. The tree house shook, quaking the pole against her back. And fear like she'd never experienced before bit into her gut.

"Cut me down! Hurry, get me down from here!" Flailing, she kicked her legs and jerked her arms against the rope. Pain shot through her wrists at the exact moment she heard the loud ripping noise above. Vince worked his hands frantically at the knots.

"Hurry, Vince, hurry!"

"I'm trying, babe," he panted, glancing up worriedly at the ceiling.

A maddening whoosh reverberated above them when the wind tore the roof from its base. The sound of cracking wood overrode that of the storm. Violent waves of cool rain splattered in on them. She screamed when a funnel of wind whipped in and lifted the oranges and mangoes, tossing them up and around the room. Ducking, she heard a sickening suction noise, and just when Vince released the last knot from her wrists, her body jerked upward—upward into the eye of the black cloud.

Tossed and tumbled, she became enveloped by cold rain, and the deafening song of wind pierced her ears. Somehow above the drone, she heard his voice far below, screaming out her name.

Chapter Nine

"*Jewel!*" Vince scrambled up the pole, his pulse pounding in his head. Quickly, he reached for her foot. But she was already gone. He looked up into the black, ominous cloud, now void of her.

"No! *Jennie, Luke!* Goddamn it. God*damn* you both." He drew back his fist and drilled it into the bamboo. Excruciating pain shot through his knuckles, up into his arm. But there could be no pain more unbearable than being without her. "How am I going to find her? Vermont—in all of fucking Vermont. Goddamn it, *how am I going to find her*, Luke, you son of a bitch?"

A current of strong air spiraled down around him. As deafening as a freight train, it tossed articles with frightening speed, reaming them at him like harpoons. He ducked and swiped angrily, batting at them as if he were in the batter's box.

"Yeah," he bellowed over the winds. "I'm pissed, too. Enough to drill you with mangoes, too, you *assholes*! Why have you two done this to us? Why?"

The reply came in the form of sudden suction. He wrapped his arms around the pole and kicked when his body rose above his head and arms. Vince held tight, gritting his teeth against the force of his anger. His biceps and triceps burned. He fought with every ounce of strength he had in him. But suddenly, it occurred to him…if he let go, maybe they'd send him to her. Maybe he'd follow the same path as Jewel.

The only way to find out was to let go.

"Luke, Jennie, I swear if you don't send me to her..." He inhaled a gust of rain-spattered, cold air. And he released the bamboo pole.

His breath caught when his body was jerked up into the black cloud. Weightless, he spun and toppled, plummeting through space and realms fraught with cold, wet darkness. With each passing minute, relaxation and grogginess fogged his mind and soul, despite the tumult of weather around him. He drew in a sharp inhalation before the deep void of unconsciousness enveloped him. And he reached for Jewel one last time, his arms coming up empty.

He dreamed of her while he floated into nothingness, the soft curves of her body, the scent of her natural perfume, the taste of her juices on his tongue. A vision of her smile and those snapping green eyes swam before him. He saw her scars, the altered little nose, the hair of a different color and length. *Jewel. She hid from you, she hurt you and she deceived you, but why?* The echo of her throaty laugh, the anger and determination in her voice, filled his ears. His brows drew together in sleep. He tossed and turned fitfully, reaching out for her, yet grasping only at turbulent air. *You've missed a big piece of the Jewel puzzle, Vince. But what? Where? How? Think, think, think...*

But he couldn't concentrate enough to find the answers. She whirled around him, spiraling, laughing wickedly, taunting and teasing him with her unique, irresistible charm. Ah, the wild passion that was only Jewel Dublin's—it seized him with a painful craving to have her in his arms once again, to sink himself into her depths.

He rolled to one side, flopped to the other, his skin wet, his clothes damp. Distantly, he became aware of a hard surface against his shoulder and hip. The air around him no longer chilled him to the bone but warmed his limbs. The darkness that had enveloped him now lightened until pale yellow light filtered through his eyelids. His body felt stiff and sore. Weak, he shoved himself over until he fell onto his back. The scent of expensive female perfume filled his nostrils with a violent rush. He curled his nose, warding off the offending odor. It wasn't Jewel's scent, it was...

"Vincie, baby, wake up." A small hand clutched at his forearm and shook him. The voice, high-pitched and babyish, grated on his nerves. "Vincie, are you all right?"

Cautiously, he opened one lid and stared into the painted face of Lucy...or was it Lacy? "No, I'm not all right."

She blinked, apparently taken aback by the bite in his tone. "Geez, sorry."

He rubbed a hand across his forehead and sat up, wincing as his muscles protested. "Sorry, Lucy. I...I must have fallen and hit my head when I answered the door."

"Laurie." Huh?

He shot a glance at her and dragged himself off the polished hardwood floor.

Her big, red, painted lips stuck out in a pout. "Huh?" "You called me Lucy. The name's Laurie." She flipped her long black hair over a tanned shoulder. Clad in nothing but a g-string, she crossed her arms under her very ample breasts. They protruded out toward him, calling, enticing. But he didn't hear or see. Snatching up a nearby throw blanket from the sofa, he wrapped it around her shoulders. She looked down with stunned appall.

"Sorry. I'm bad with names. Um, listen, I…I really need to get back to work…if you don't mind. Do you think you could…?"

"Oh, thank God you're awake!" The sweet feminine drawl came from behind him. "I was just looking for your phone to call an ambulance. Man, Vince, you were out cold!"

Vince turned to see the petite, small-breasted little beauty stroll from his bedroom—naked. Candy…or Katy? he wondered. Either way, she apparently wasn't a true blonde, he thought as his gaze fell to the black landing strip between her legs. How had he not noticed that? He'd sunk his cock right there below that neatly trimmed patch, and still, he hadn't noticed—or cared, he thought with surprise—about all the little details.

"I was? For how long?" He flicked a look toward the massive patio door. Judging by the slant of the sunrays bathing the condominiums across the street, it was mid-afternoon. He whirled toward the fireplace and focused on the mantel clock. One thirty-five.

"Who cares how long? Let's go, Kelly." Laurie spun on her heel and headed for the bedroom—and her clothes, obviously. "The fun's over. Our prince charming apparently has turned back into a fricking nasty old frog."

"What?" Kelly—Vince noted her real name this time—paused in stunned confusion. "Go? Why? We're supposed to spend the whole weekend with him."

"Yeah, well, it looks like," Laurie spoke from the other room, her voice muffled as she donned her clothes, "that's no longer the case."

"Now, wait," Vince croaked. God, when did he ever worry about a woman's feelings? And why did he long to lose this argument just to be alone with his thoughts of...a woman by the sea. The chant suddenly filled his mind the way one of those songs on the radio did, the kind that played over and over in your head and wouldn't stop. "I— I didn't mean to come off as a—"

"Jerk?" Laurie asked when she sailed into the room clothed in a black leather skirt and little satin blouse. Her hair flew behind her in a cloud of angry, silky midnight.

"Jerk," Vince agreed. He plopped down on the sofa and stared at the ceiling.

Kelly slithered down next to him. Her perfume, warm and mixed with the scent of pussy, wrapped around him along with her slim arms. She kissed his neck, his cheek, his mouth. "He's not a jerk," she purred, winking one thickly mascaraed eye at him. "He just needs to jerk off...with our help."

He shook his head, even as she cupped his balls and rolled them around in her palm. Practiced, she slithered her hand up and wrapped it around his soft cock through the boxers he wore once again. Nothing. Not one ache stirred in his loins.

"No, I'm sorry, but that's the last thing I need right now." He took her hand and gently removed it from his crotch.

Kelly's bleached eyebrows arched. But it didn't take long for dawning to light her brown eyes. Those same eyebrows inverted angrily. "Hey, what's up with you? This isn't the man we picked up in the stripper bar last night. Did you get a concussion or something?"

He had to laugh at that. "Yes." Vince rubbed his head, feigning a headache. "I think I got a *major* concussion. And I'm not feeling so well. Look," he rushed on and stood up, glancing between the two artificial beauties. "Something's wrong here. I went to answer the door this morning and must have passed out. I think I need to go see a doctor."

"Oh yes, a shrink, maybe." Laurie obviously wasn't the forgiving type. She snatched up her teeny black purse and marched over to Kelly. "Go get dressed. We're leaving." With a withering stare at Vince, she added, "And we're never coming back again."

Kelly shot to her feet so fast, even her tiny breasts jiggled. "All right," she hissed. "Give me a minute. I'm right behind you." She marched into the bedroom, her brassy, fake blonde hair swishing across her naked ass. He noted the dark roots and thought of Jewel. Funny that she'd dyed her hair black, as if to hide her true beauty, while this woman had bleached hers blonde in order to flare up her looks.

Vince sighed. "Look, I'm really sorry—"

Laurie held up a hand. She was already standing in the open door that led out to the corridor. "Don't *even* give us the softy routine. We know your type. Funny," she sniffed haughtily as Kelly emerged and stood in the doorway with her. "You came off as such a nice guy last night. Unusual for a man in a strip bar. But we made a terrible mistake," she sneered, slanting a look down his body. "You're just like all the other assholes."

"Ouch."

"Damn right, ouch. Now," she went on, jutting her chin toward the dining room table. "Go drink some of that fancy champagne you stingily hid from us last night and go fuck off and die."

Vince startled when the door slammed. "Great." With a mixed groan of relief and guilt, he dropped to the cushions and plucked up the cordless on the table behind the sofa. Yep, he needed to see a doctor—and maybe even a shrink as Laurie had so eloquently suggested.

Deciding to check his voice messages first, he dialed the access number and entered his password. Reaching for a pad and pen, he listened and jotted down the four numbers for clients he needed to get back with very soon. Next came the calls that had apparently been recorded yesterday evening during his night out on the town.

"Hello, hot stuff," the female voice purred. "This is Steffy—who else?" she added with a girlie laugh. "I've got some time off, photo shoot's done a day early. Call me."

The sweet, soft voice of Melanie the professional skier came next. "Well, howdy, hunk! Hey, where you been? I left a message yesterday and you haven't called me back yet. I hope everything's okay. I was able to finagle a suite at the Alpine Ski Resort for next weekend, just like you suggested. Let me know…"

"Vince Santiago, it's your lucky day. We're going to be in town for a two-day filming this Thursday and Friday. My character's part will only take one of those two days to shoot. So guess what? You get an early birthday present." The sound of a sexy, expectant sigh filled his ears. "Call me as soon as you get in. Here's my new cell phone number…"

He warred with himself over how to respond to each of these messages. Rolling his eyes, he plopped his bare feet up on the glass coffee table and made note of each.

He'd have to do the gentlemanly thing, he supposed, and at least call them all back to cancel.

"Vince, you're pathetic. A real fucking loser," he snarled to himself, still holding the phone to his ear as the recording prompted the date and time of another incoming message.

"Hello, Vince." The familiar voice in his ear drew a gasp from him. He sat up on the edge of the sofa, his feet hitting the wooden floor with a slap. "It's Jennie. When you finally get through beating yourself over the head, go on over to the dining room table and open that bottle Laurie—or is it Lucy?—suggested you drink."

He hadn't bothered to look and see what Laurie had been referring to. All he'd wanted, he realized with a silent self-scolding, was for her to shut up and leave. His gaze snapped across the vaulted room to the corner where his glass dining table sat. He peered between the richly upholstered, high-backed dining chairs.

And there it was. *The bottle.*

"Oh, no. Oh, no..."

"Oh, yes, Vince." Even though it was a recording, Vince didn't notice Jennie replied as if she spoke directly to him. "Go. Go over and open it."

"No. Not again."

"Do you want to see her again?"

His heart palpated hungrily. "Of course I do."

"Then open it."

He punched the button and tossed the cordless handset onto the couch. Never taking his eyes from the bottle, he rose and slowly crossed the room. All he could think of was Jewel, Jewel, Jewel. If he opened the bottle, would she materialize before him? Would she appear so they could, once and for all, get things untangled and move on with their future?

There was only one way to find out. With a sure and steady hand, he reached out and plucked up the bottle. This time, it didn't induce him with horniness as it had before. But he didn't care. He had only one motivation in mind.

Getting Jewel back.

Clutching the neck in one hand and the glittering stopper in the other, he yanked off the top. A familiar breeze laced with hibiscus and coconut filled his nostrils. Pale, lavender-tinged smoke filled the room. When it dissipated, it left behind...Jennie. She stood there, petite and proud and beautiful in a shimmering navy chiffon toga. Both of her upper arms were ringed with wide gold bands shaped like fern leaves. On her head, she wore a gold, jeweled headdress that lent her a regal, almost haughty air. All but two white wisps framing her face were swept up into the crown. Though her breasts were twin swells of womanly perfection, and her body that of a goddess, he paid not the least bit of attention.

"Where is she?"

Jennie smiled and sat on...air. He shook his head with irritation, watching as she floated five feet above the floor, her legs folded Indian-style. "My, but you're an impatient one."

He took two steps toward her, his teeth ground together. "Jennie, don't tempt me to wrap my hands around your pretty neck."

She flicked a hand. Vince smacked into an invisible panel. Anger glittered in her eyes, though she continued to smile sweetly. "Don't tempt me to hide her from you forever."

All he could do was sigh. Setting the bottle down on the dining table with a clink, he replied, "You know I don't want that."

"Yes. I'm aware of that."

He yanked out a chair and collapsed onto its firm, damask-covered surface. His mind snapped with an odd irritation. He hated this table and chairs. Why had he purchased such a snooty, uncomfortable, impractical set? Annoyed with himself, he shoved aside the place setting that hadn't been used since being placed there years ago. Dusted around, washed by his maid, maybe, but never once used.

"What now? You said to open the bottle if I wanted to see her again."

"Ah, I *implied* you'd see her again if you opened it. Two entirely different things."

"What do you want from me? You took me through that ridiculous dream. I've been gone for what seemed like days but it turned out only to be hours."

"It was days on Carnal Island—two-and-a-half, in fact. And you call seeing the woman you love ridiculous?"

He paused, staring up at her for a long moment. It had to be a trick question. She'd mentioned love in the beginning, when she'd first popped into his life. Now here it was again.

"Love?"

"You love her. Why else do you think you've been putting yourself through all this shallow torture the last four years?"

"Shallow torture?"

She nodded and stretched out on her side, planting her fist against her temple. "Yes, like with your Lucy or Lacy, and Candy or Katy."

"Laurie and Kelly," he corrected.

"Whatever. And then there's all this...stiffness you continue to surround yourself with. Now," she said, sitting up so quickly, he had to jerk his head up. "Do you want to see her or not?"

He leapt to his feet. The chair toppled over behind him, cracking on the wood floor. "Goddamn it, I said I do, and you know I do, whether I tell you or not!" He glared at her and yanked the chair up, righting it.

"Then admit how you feel, Vince. I know where she is. I know exactly where she is. And this is just getting downright ludicrous how you're both only able to speak clearly to each other with your bodies. Nonetheless, I'm not spilling any jelly beans until you finally let go of that pig-headed pride of yours and admit that you can't admit you love her because you're still pissed at her after four years!"

He stared at her for what seemed like eons. How was it that he was standing here arguing with a fucking genie when he totally agreed with every word the sneaky wench spoke?

Pride.

Had he really been feeding on his damn pride for four years? A vision of Jewel swam before his eyes, both new and old. He thought of all those days, weeks, months and years he'd been miserable without her, trying to talk himself into this rich, playboy lifestyle to forget her. Shallow torture, Jennie had called it. He snorted. And she was right. What a better way to bury her, to forget how she'd shredded his heart to pieces by walking out on him? She'd demanded he state his intentions of marriage to her before he'd even gotten the nerve up to ask her to move in with him. She'd hurt him beyond what he thought a man should ever have to feel or be forced to admit to. She'd walked out on him and hadn't returned his calls, the rejection further fueling his obstinacy. But there had been a good reason...the accident. That goddamn male pride of his had been the sole obstacle all these years. He could have easily gone to Celeste and demanded to know Jewel's whereabouts, or called her brother in Colorado Springs. But instead, he'd allowed his stubborn vanity to torture him into a shallow lifestyle that completely negated his past relationship with Jewel.

How self-deprecating was that?

"Oh, fuck me," he groaned and buckled back into the chair.

* * * * *

"Jewel, honey...are you all right?"

Warm flesh pressed against her forehead. Jewel opened her eyes slow and cautious. Her vision blurred momentarily, and she inhaled the convent's familiar scent of mustiness and mothballs. The light of afternoon sun poured in behind the nun, making her glow angelically.

"Sister Neoma?"

"Yes, dear." The wrinkled face with the sharp blue eyes stared back at her amid the black circle of the habit. "We'd begun to worry about you. I know it's Saturday, but normally you come down for breakfast. When you didn't show for lunch, too, I thought I'd best check on you. Hmm..." Her silver eyebrows dipped. She blotted Jewel's face and neck above the gown with a washcloth. "You're drenched. Yet you don't appear to be running a fever. Do you feel ill, child?"

Ill? Yes, quite. Everything came rushing back to her in a whirlwind that made her head spin with sudden nausea. Carnal Island, being stranded and reduced to a heathen…Vince. *God, please don't let it be only a dream!*

"Jewel?"

She blinked. "What?"

"I said do you feel ill?" She scowled. "Hmm, your skin, it's…it's almost as if you've been out in the sun."

"Oh, no," she assured Neoma, sitting up to prove her point. Brief dizziness washed over her, but she planted her hand on the hard mattress determined to right herself. "I'm…I'm fine. And my skin…I must have gotten some sun when I took the children on that field trip into the woods. Whew. I had a very long, strange dream, and I guess I was extra tired and—"

She cut herself off, unable to believe her eyes.

"What's the matter, dear?" Neoma hooked an arm about Jewel's shoulders and drew her into a grandmotherly embrace, leaning to peer into her face.

Jewel swallowed, unblinking. Her eyes held hard and tight to the bottle sitting on her dresser. She stood slowly, very carefully so the apparition wouldn't disappear. "Where did that come from?"

Neoma swiveled her head as sharply as she could in the confining habit. "Why, I don't know. I assumed you'd bought yourself a fancy bottle of wine to share during communion. It's not yours?"

Jewel, you know very well where it came from. Now get rid of her so we can talk.

She gasped. "Luke? Is that you?"

"Luke who?" Neoma asked, her eyes clouding with confusion. "Child, are you sure you're all right? I could call the house infirmary and see if the doctor is still about."

"No!"

Neoma startled and backed two steps toward the door. "Why, Jewel, honey, you're really starting to worry me. I've never seen you act so bizarre and look so wild-eyed. Lord God, I pray you're not coming down with something"—she tapped her temple—"of the mind-sort."

You're wasting time, Ms. Dublin. Precious time.

"Oh, just shut up for one moment, would you?" Jewel darted her gaze around the tiny room, up to the ceiling, into each corner, behind her. She could hear Luke as clearly as if he stood right next to her, but he had yet to materialize.

"I beg your pardon?" Neoma gasped.

"No, not you, Sister. Do you hear that? A man speaking to me?"

"God is speaking to you?" Her face brightened with hope.

Jewel couldn't help but laugh. "No, he's most certainly not God."

A swift breeze blew in, tossing the curtains wildly. *I am too a god!*

"Okay, *a* god, but not *the* God."

Neoma stumbled backward until she crashed into the wooden door. Never taking her eyes from Jewel, she fumbled behind her back for the doorknob. "Lord God in heaven, you're possessed!" She crossed her chest and mumbled something Jewel couldn't discern. Her hands shook as she held them pressed together before her mouth in prayer. "Jesus, help us all."

Luke chuckled. *Possessed with a voracious sexual appetite, maybe.*

"Luke, if you don't shut up so I can explain to Neoma—" The slam of the door severed her words. "Now look what you've gone and done. She thinks I'm a crazy woman possessed by the devil. How am I going to explain *that*? I have to work here, you know."

Quit delaying and open the bottle. We have some very important things to discuss, which I despise doing from inside this damn bottle. Now let me out of here.

She snorted, even as she rose to go do his bidding. "Ah, the control I have. How I'd love to make you stay in there for eternity."

Don't even—

Jewel yanked the stopper, watching unfazed when a poof of gray smoke filled the room. As it dissipated, the flesh and blood of Luke Slayton appeared before her. She let out a sigh of relief. Maybe, just maybe he could do some of his hocus-pocus and put her right back in Vince's arms.

"Think about leaving me in there," Luke finished his statement, his thick arms crossed over his chest. He wore one of those silly-looking Greek togas again, yet there was nothing silly about the way it emphasized his physique. But the only man's build she was interested in was that of a man who'd dumped her in the most emotional time of a woman's life. The thought of it still pained raw and fresh in her soul.

"Well, now that you've succeeded in most likely getting me fired, then probably followed by involuntary commitment to a mental institution, and a grueling exorcism, please, feel free to talk all you want," Jewel replied saucily.

He stepped nearer and she caught the scent of coconut and forest. It immediately brought back memories of her stay on Carnal Island...and Vince's fiery lovemaking.

He didn't waste time with the topic. "You want him, Jewel. You know you do."

She tossed her head, trying desperately to rid her heart of the wistfulness that invaded it. "You got me there. I can't deny it. You saw yourself how he turns me on, how he makes me feel. The physical attraction between us can't be denied. That's never changed, obviously, and never will. But that isn't a good enough basis for a relationship— for forever, which is what I wanted from the start."

He rolled his eyes and hitched himself up on the dresser next to his bottle. Dangling his feet, bumping his sandals against the drawers, he gripped the edge and leaned toward her. His aqua eyes snared her, making her think of a tropical breeze, a kiss, a stolen moment of passion. With Vince.

"Didn't you learn anything on Carnal Island?"

"Okay, so you tried to teach me some sort of lesson there. Well, I'm sorry, but I fail to see where you've gone with this. I fail to see how throwing Vince on an island with me—when he didn't want me in the first damn place—is helpful to your cause. Love cannot be forced. That's all there is to it, Luke." She paced before him, now and then snapping her gaze back to him. She didn't care that he stared at her with that smug look. She needed to get it all off her chest. Now.

"I want him to love me, but only of his own free will. That's why I walked out on him in the first place. I couldn't stick around trying to finagle a drop here and a smidgen there of love out of him. It had to be genuine for what I was about to spring on him, and love and what all goes with love, weren't part of his big plan. Just sex and a little fun until the next woman came along. That's what his big strategy had been all those years ago. And I found that out when I was forced to ask him his intentions — which I needed to know *before* I dropped the big bomb on him."

"You're not telling me anything I don't already know, Jewel. But I can tell you some things *you* don't know. Here." He snapped his fingers. "First, you must watch your past, right here on the Xanthian Big Screen."

She abruptly ceased her steps and stared at him with incredulity. "Xanthian? What are you...?"

Luke's voice began to echo in her head. Her eyes widened when a huge, flat panel appeared before her. Like a giant video screen, it showed her her life with Vince, in horrid, emotional details that it seemed she'd missed at the time. Luke confirmed to her in movie-fashion on the screen, what had really happened. And this time, she listened, she watched closely and she finally understood.

"See there how he hounded you with messages that entire week you were hospitalized after the accident?" A picture of Vince, handsome, his brow worried, filled the screen. "Now, you didn't return his calls, of course, because you couldn't. But he was frantic, heartbroken by what he thought was your blatant, permanent rejection of him for not proposing a future with you, for not telling you what you'd wanted to hear during that final argument. But your best friend, your roommate Celeste...watch there as she deletes all of his messages."

And Celeste did, indeed, appear before her, her jaw set with anger on Jewel's behalf as she punched angrily at the delete button. "On your erratic drive home from Vince's apartment in Denver, before the accident, remember you called her on your cell phone?"

"Yes," Jewel whispered, her eyes filling with tears as that scene played out before her. She watched herself tremble, the tears pouring from her eyes as she dialed the phone while driving in a rainstorm. The car swerved, she jerked it back on the road. All she'd wanted was to die if she couldn't be with him anymore.

Luke went on. "You relayed to Celeste how you'd dumped him right before he'd dumped you, how much of a jerk he was, how you never wanted to see him again, how you were done with him forever. And you cried with the pain of lost love."

Yes, she remembered all too well the pain of it, the stubborn determination to punish him for rejecting her. For not wanting to marry her right away. She watched herself pour out her heart to her friend over the phone as she drove in the thunderstorm, sailing too fast over slick roads.

All along, she realized, she'd been punishing them both. How could that possibly be love? she thought, hating herself for not seeing it before now. You cannot expect to gain someone's love and a lifetime commitment if you're making such demands out of the blue and not explaining your motivation. Why hadn't she seen it before? Why had she always made him out to be the cad, when all along, she'd been the one to suddenly disrupt a blooming relationship?

She shook her head, focusing on the screen. Tears blazed in her eyes. In horrid detail, she watched herself pump on the brake as an unexpected sharp curve loomed before her. Rain spattered on the windshield too quickly to clear her line of vision, even with the wipers on high speed. Her headlights sliced through the forest to her left, and suddenly, she was screaming, the car plunging over the cliff into a ravine. She could feel the sharp sensations even now as she studied the movie. There was the crash of shattering glass, the excruciating pain ripping through her abdomen and the final burst of agony in her head as her face hit the windshield and she blacked out. She watched herself slump against the wheel, blood spattered in a sickening shower over her mangled face, her shattered nose, throughout the interior of the car.

"When you had this horrible, disfiguring accident, you were unconscious for many, many days. You couldn't return his calls, and in fact, you didn't know about them. Celeste had informed your family of Vince's supposed rejection, so they, in turn, rejected him by not notifying him of your condition. And Celeste, meanwhile, also deleted those messages and refused, for your sake—or so she thought—to take the initiative and call him to report where you were. She never told you what she'd done, and not done, as well. She loved you and thought you'd be better off in your oblivion without the man you'd painted as an ogre in her eyes."

The scene flipped to Celeste, her brunette head lowered in anger, as she once again punched the delete button on the machine. Vince had told her the truth. He'd called time after time, but she never knew. And he hadn't known she'd had the horrible accident. During that emotional confession session in the tree house on Carnal Island, she'd thought him to be a liar, a heartless asshole. And she'd silently claimed to love him?

The screen switched then, to Vince, frustration and bewilderment clear on his handsome face as he lowered the phone to the cradle for the twentieth time that week. He closed his eyes on a heart-wrenching sigh.

"Jewel, sweetheart... Where are you? Why are you doing this to me? I miss you. I...I have to see you. We need to talk. Y-you don't understand. I just need time, but not without you."

And he hadn't gotten one word from her. She hadn't returned one call, and he'd obviously been as devastated by her rejection as she had by his.

"Had you just trusted him more," Luke went on, almost in a rush, Jewel thought, "and gone on to tell him about your secret news that night, he'd have come around. He was already toying with the idea of letting go of his bachelorhood, of possibly settling down, and marriage, after a trial run of living together, of course. True, your sudden interrogation of him had scared the shit out of him, but that's just Vince Santiago. He needs time to come to his own terms in his own mind, to be sure it's what's best for everyone, and what he really wants — without being influenced by persuasive tears, accusations...and a woman's allure. Vince has his faults, and his pride certainly hadn't allowed him to pursue you beyond that first week, but to him, you'd walked out on him for good. Forever. Once he came to terms with that, his own stubbornness took over, followed by a playboy lifestyle he'd rather have been spending with you."

Tears streamed down her face. She watched as the movie screen flipped to Vince in his apartment. Jennie hovered nearby, and Jewel listened to their whole exchange. She stared agog as he leapt up from a richly upholstered dining chair.

She heard Jennie chastising him. "Then admit how you feel, Vince. I know where she is. I know exactly where she is. And this is just getting downright ludicrous how you're both only able to speak clearly to each other with your bodies. Nonetheless, I'm not spilling any jelly beans until you finally let go of that pig-headed pride of yours and admit that you can't admit you love her because you're still pissed at her after four years!"

Vince's face went pale. He stood there stunned, then dropped back into the chair. "Oh, fuck me," he groaned. For a long moment, he held his head in his hands, rubbing his face raw. "I *am* a stubborn bastard. All this time wasted. And all I probably had to do was go find her and tell her I love her. That I've loved her all along."

Jewel stumbled backward and collapsed to the bed, the room spinning around her. All those years, all those long years of hating him, wanting him, loving him yet refusing to contact him, wasted. Months and years of keeping that tormenting secret buried and to herself, and fleeing to another corner of the country. She'd wasted all this time in this place, practically holding herself prisoner. She'd even considered pursuing a lifetime commitment to the nunnery in order to finally cleanse Vince from her soul. Nausea swirled in her gut and she pressed a hand to her belly. Glancing around at the drab, tiny room, listening to the deafening silence beyond that rickety door... Holy shit, how had she endured it? All those years lost and so very lonely, when all she'd had to do was reach out to Vince, to tell the truth and be honest just as the nuns always preached. And just as she had preached countless times to the children in her classroom.

This whole mix-up was all her fault, all due to her stubborn pride and childish need to punish him. And he'd loved her all along!

"Oh, God. He loves me. And I love him, yet I never told him out of fear of rejection. He doesn't even know it." She rubbed her stomach to still the butterflies. Giddy, she giggled, sure that if Neoma heard her, she'd have her thrown into a straightjacket. *"He loves me, Luke! He loves me!"*

Luke sighed. "Yes, that's what we've been trying to prove to you all along...with a little help from some healthy bouts of sex, of course."

"Of course." Jewel couldn't help but smile.

A thought suddenly occurred to her. She stood up slowly. "I have to tell him everything, don't I?"

"Hot damn, Xanthus, I think she's got it!"

Unable to help herself, she chuckled softly. "Luke?"

"Yes?"

"Why didn't you just tell me all this from the start, instead of putting me on that island with him? It would have saved a lot of time and grief."

He let out a sarcastic cluck of the tongue. "Picture this... Bottle suddenly appears out of the dawn." He waved his hands dramatically. "Hot, handsome genie materializes before Jewel's very eyes. She's utterly disbelieving and assumes she's hallucinating. Studly genie says, 'Oh, by the way, Vince Santiago has always loved you. Go ahead, pack up and head on out to Denver for a happily-ever-after. Bye, now!' Now tell me truthfully, would you have gone to Denver? Really?"

Jewel blinked. "Well, of course not."

He began to float, his body now reclining. "If I'd have suggested a getaway on a hedonistic island, and presented you with airline tickets and an itinerary, would the almost-nun, prim and prideful Jewel Dublin, have gone?"

"No, but—"

"And if I'd have told the then haughty, very bitter Jewel Dublin, that the man she loved and yet hated with her entire soul would be there as her only companion for a full two to three days, would she have gone?"

"Okay. You make some good points." She blew out a breath of resignation. "I would have told you to go to hell and get out of my dream."

"Bingo! So you had to be 'abducted', as you once called it, and made to see the error of your stubborn ways. But Vince had his issues, too, so don't feel alone in this, hon."

She snorted. "Thanks for the reminder."

"Well," he said, sitting up to brush his palms together in a task-complete gesture. "That just about does it. Except for one thing."

"Yes?"

"Let's get you out of that *dreary* gown and into something hot."

Chapter Ten

Jewel nodded her agreement. "Hurry. Please hurry."

"Jewel, sweetheart, you can just bet I will. Whether you know it or not, the clock's been ticking for us all."

With a wave of his hand and a simple chant, the task was complete. She looked down to find herself clad in a very revealing, very short and sexy, see-through black negligee. Already, her pussy was getting wet just thinking about Vince seeing her this way. She turned this way and that, sticking out one foot to examine the shoes. High, spiky, red stiletto heels decorated her feet, making her heart pound with anticipation. She angled toward the dresser mirror and studied the effect Luke had conjured up. Her hair had been swept up into a clip, and seductive, golden wisps and curls framed her face, now highlighted with red lipstick and just a touch of eye makeup. "Wow. He's gonna flip."

"That's the idea, hon." Luke grinned wolfishly, clearly enjoying this matchmaking game he played.

"I have to go to him. As soon as possible." She crossed the room and took Luke's hand. It felt large and warm and friendly in hers. "Can you help me? Can you…you know, do some more abracadabra or something, and send me to him? Like right now?"

"You bet. Now that you've both admitted your love for each other, I can do all the magic I want." He lifted her hand and gave the back of it a loud, smacking kiss.

"Where do you want to go? To his place? To Carnal Island? Anywhere you want to go, hon."

She inhaled swiftly and her heart fluttered at the thought of seeing Vince again so soon. "Can we?"

"Can you what?"

"Go back to Carnal Island?" The thought of spending time with him there to hash everything out, to make up for all those lost years, made her system thrum with eagerness. Already, she could feel her clit throbbing beneath the hem of the negligee.

"Honey, you've helped my soul mate to earn one of two needed wings, so to speak. So yes. If Carnal Island is your desire, consider it done. We'd be honored to have you both as guests once again at our exciting, catered, all-inclusive resort."

"All-inclusive?"

"All-inclusive."

"But...but we didn't see any resort on Carnal Island. It was deserted, completely abandoned."

"Really?" Suddenly evasive, he turned his back on her, floated to the window and parted the curtain.

"Really. Um, Luke?"

"Hmm?" He didn't turn, only looked down upon the courtyard of the convent.

"So all that time we struggled to survive, there was really a civilized resort nearby?"

He spun and presented her with his most charming, devastating smile. "Well, of course. Carnal Island is and can be all things to all people in need. Depending on what their particular situation is in need of, of course."

"Of course." She couldn't suppress the grin that spread across her face, but still tapped her foot and folded her arms, snaring him with a scolding look. Nonetheless, joy filled her heart. Looking back, there would have been no way two people would have been able to fill such a deep rift while being wined and dined on pâté and caviar. Not if those two people were as stubborn and prideful as she and Vince were.

Luke glanced away guiltily. "So, do you want to go or not?"

She flew across the room, her stilettos clomping on the wood floor, and threw her arms around him. "Thank you, Luke. Thank you and Jennie, both." She cupped his face in her hands and planted a loud, smacking kiss on his stunned lips. "Now, let's get the hell out of here before the nuns come and throw me into a paddy wagon."

* * * * *

Vince tried his best to relax in the lounge chair, waiting, hoping to see her again. He still couldn't believe all this civilized pampering had been just out of reach those two days or so that he and Jewel had struggled to survive. Perplexed, he shook his head, certain he'd covered the island from shore to shore.

He scanned the palm tree-dotted area below the balcony where couples engaged in various carnal activities around a huge swimming pool and waterfall. A tiki bar set on the edge of the shallow end was lined with underwater barstools. Naked men and women sat on them engaging in lazy sexual play as they sipped piña coladas and strawberry margaritas. Nude volleyball and miniature golf were in full swing. The sound of flirty giggles, both distant and near carried on the sultry air. Inhaling hungrily, Vince could smell pineapple and glazed ham roasting on the beach below where The Catch restaurant prepared for a luau. The sun blazed overhead, soaking already-bronzed skin with hot rays. Off in the distance, white-tipped waves rolled in from the Gulf, the rush of their eager flight crashing ashore. Sea gulls swooped over a school of groupers, squawking in frustration when they snagged a kill, only to have the fish slip from their beaks and flop back into the water.

He tipped his beer and swallowed a long draught. It slid down his throat icy-cold and fizzy. Vince plucked up a lemon slice from the snack tray room service had placed on the patio table, and chased his beer with a suck of the tart pulp. On a whim, he riffled through the lime slices and popped a fat one into his beer. And with a sigh, he closed his eyes, laced the bottle in his hands over his belly and tried to relax.

"Hello, Vince."

His eyelids popped open. The sound of her voice filled his ears, sweet and seductive. He sat upright and swiveled his head toward the sound, unsure if he'd imagined it.

And there she stood in the opening of the sliding glass door to his suite.

"Jewel." It came out on a sighed groan. He set the beer down absently and rose, his eyes never leaving her.

Curtains fluttered around her in the tropical breeze, and her alluring scent floated across the space, instantly putting his dick on alert inside his cut-off jean shorts. The upswept style of her hair made him long to run his fingers through it and release the glossy tresses so they bounced around her bare shoulders. Her eyes had been accented with a faint touch of makeup, just enough to make a man long to drown in those glittering gems. His gaze fell to the mouth, painted in kissable cherry-red and curved in a soft but seductive smile. His heart skipped a beat when his shocked brain finally registered what she wore. The black, sheer, lacy little number emphasized every curve and every plane of her voluptuous body. He noted how her faintly bronzed skin glittered in the sunlight, emphasizing the deep cavern of her cleavage where the old crone's silver necklace still nestled. Zippers and buttons had been sewn into strategic spots that made his fingers curl with need to undo them all. He slid a look down over the vee where he could see the outline of moist lips. His pulse galloped through his system, stirring up heat and making his cock tingle with the rise of an inevitable erection. With rigid control, he imagined yanking aside that silky strip and sinking himself into her dampness, feeling her tight muscles clamp around him.

Or better yet, he thought, licking his lips, he'd like to lap up every drop of that delicious cream of hers and *then* bury his shaft into her. Unable to remove his gaze from her, still visually hungry, he shifted his perusal lower. The long length of toned legs poured into red, high-heeled shoes the exact shade as her lipstick. He'd never seen her in fuck-me heels like this before. In fact, he'd never seen her in a negligee like this before. The novelty of it assaulted his libido with deadly accuracy.

Unable to help himself, he let out a long, low whistle. "Holy shit."

"Is that all you have to say? 'Holy shit'?" She slinked forward, her breasts jiggling enticingly. "Not very romantic, Vincent Santiago."

"Jewel...I—oh God, you're here. You came back to me."

She nodded and stopped in front of him, the heels bringing her almost eyelevel with him. The tempting fragrance of floral perfume and pussy filled his lungs. "We have a lot to discuss."

His palms itched to feel her satiny flesh. He set them on her shoulders and slid his hands downward, soaking in the softness of her flesh. Twining his hands with hers, he replied, "I'm so sorry for being so stubborn, and for hurting you that way. I...I guess I was scared when you demanded to know if I had intentions of marrying you. But, Jewel," he said, squeezing her hands, "it didn't mean I didn't want you. It didn't mean I didn't love you. Marriage would have come in its own time."

She smiled softly and planted a butterfly kiss on his mouth. The flavor of love and forgiveness burst in his mouth. "I know that now, Vince. And I'm sorry I forced myself on you like that and then walked out. I felt like you'd totally rejected me. I thought you didn't want me and our—" She halted her words abruptly, her lids squeezing shut.

"What, sweetheart? Our what?" He tipped her chin up so that she was forced to open her eyes and look into his.

Tears glittered over emerald pools. He watched as the sun glinted off each droplet. They spilled over, soft and pure, and rolled down her cheeks. "Our baby," she whispered.

Our *baby*?

Stunned, her words slammed into him with unexpected force. He swallowed a lump that threatened to choke him to death. Shaking his head frantically, he tried desperately to clear every sound from his ears but that of her words. "Did you say our...baby?"

"Yes."

"I have a baby?"

"No."

"What? Wait. You're not making any sense." He collapsed onto the lounge chair, his elbows resting on his knees as he looked up into her beautiful, tormented face. "I...I don't understand."

She squatted down and her slightly spread legs afforded him a perfect view of her vee. But he couldn't concentrate on that right now, no matter how alluring the sight. He lifted his gaze to hers. She planted a hand on his cheek, cool and gentle. Her eyes bored into his, begging for understanding.

"I'd just found out I was pregnant. It was why I came to you that night with this sudden need to know your intentions. The last thing I wanted was for you to marry me just because I was pregnant. I needed to know if you really loved me, if you really had plans, even if very long-term, to spend the rest of your life with me. I couldn't tell you, at least not at the moment, until I knew for sure, because I didn't want to be a charity case for you. I wanted to be wanted first, loved first. It had to be that way for me *before* I told you about the baby. A child needs, in my opinion, a strong foundation of parents that truly love each other first. Do you understand?"

He couldn't stop shaking his head. His stomach fluttered with the reality of what had truly happened. Flashes of what she'd said, how irrational and frantic she'd acted, moved through his memory. It all started to come together, to become crystal-clear. Except for one thing.

"You said you were pregnant, but that I don't have a baby. Jewel, please tell me you didn't..."

Sobs tore from her. She laid her head in his lap and collapsed to her knees. "No, I didn't. I could never give up your child for any reason in any way. The wreck. I told you about the wreck. I lost the baby, Vince. I miscarried our child that very night because of the accident, and I woke up from that coma devastated that I'd lost you both."

Dazed, he could swear his heart stopped. The thought of her going through all that emotional and physical pain all alone without him, crushed him completely. Guilt reached out to slap him across the face and punch him in the gut.

He gathered her close, clutching her to him. "I'm so sorry, Jewel. God, I'm *so* sorry!" Tears stung his eyes and he shut them tight, allowing the wetness to cleanse his cheeks and his heart.

Her arms wound around him, squeezing with sincere forgiveness and comfort. "No, Vince, we're both to blame." She reared back and framed his face in her hands, forcing him to look into her soul. And he thought she'd never looked stronger and more beautiful in all the years he'd known her.

"You see, for me," she went on, "hurt and pain turned to anger, which further complicated it. After I'd gone through all the surgeries and lost all that weight due to having to have my jaw wired shut, I sought you out one night. You were in a bar having the time of your life. Women were draped all over you. I hated you at that moment. I wondered how I could love a man so much who didn't love me back. And so I left without even bothering to confront you or explain what I'd been through."

"And because of Celeste, you thought I'd dumped you completely."

She nodded eagerly, and he could see in her eyes how the therapy of finally talking about it gave her relief and hope. "Yes. So I found a teaching job in the convent in Vermont and vowed to become a nun so I could cleanse you from my system. Silly, I know, but I needed desperately to forget all that I had had, and that had been taken away from me in such a short time. I couldn't go on without you. It seemed my only way, at the time, of getting through life without cracking up."

"Oh, baby," he breathed, kissing her forehead, her wet cheeks, her mouth. "It kills me to think you went through all that pain and suffering without me. I want to make it up to you. Will you let me?"

She beamed through her tears, and her answer came out on a choked cry. "I'm counting on it, Santiago."

He dragged her up and turned her so that she sat on the lounge chair next to him. Rising, he dropped to one knee. "I'm supposed to be the one down on my knees," he grinned ruefully.

Her mouth fell open. She stared at him through eyes that sparkled with stunned faith. "What...what are you doing?"

He closed his eyes and breathed in her sultry scent. God, how he wanted that smell around him forever! "I'm proposing to you."

She slapped a hand over that blood-red mouth. "Are you serious?"

His grin faded. He reached into his pocket and drew out a black velvet box laden with a silver lock. "The key, Jewel. I need your key."

Confused, she stared into his eyes. Following his gaze downward, she looked at the chain that still hung around her neck. "This?"

He nodded. "It's the key to your heart. Inside, is the key to mine, just like the old witch said on the beach that day."

Understanding dawned on her gorgeous face. She lifted the chain over her head, her expression dazed when the encrusted ruby on its surface glowed in her hand.

Vince turned the box's lock toward her. "Unlock my heart, Jewel. Forever."

Without hesitation, she inserted the silver key into the lock. She gasped in delight when the lid popped open. The sun glinted down on a two-carat, platinum-gold diamond ring nestled in white satin.

"It's the band the old crone slipped on your finger that day!" she rasped, fighting tears of joy.

Yes, he thought, one and the same ring. Only now, the symbol of love and the promise of forever nestled within prongs that stood proud and strong. The diamond she would wear for the rest of their lives winked at him, taking his breath away.

"Jewel Dublin, will you marry me?"

She threw her arms around him and shrieked, "Yes. Oh my God, *yes*, Vinnie!"

A breeze blew in cool and strong. It carried with it the scent of tropical blooms just perfect for a wedding. Vince knew Jennie and Luke looked on, and somehow, it pleased him that his old college buddy turned genie, and his gorgeous genie wife, had shared this tender moment with them.

He slipped the ring on her finger and watched, his heart pumping sure and sturdy, as she turned her hand this way and that, taking in every cut and angle of the diamond.

"Happy?"

She glanced up, her eyes snaring him with an overflow of emotions. "Ecstatic. Vince," she sighed, sliding her arms around his neck. "I love you. I've always loved you. And I'm so glad I woke up one morning to find a strange bottle on my dresser at the convent."

He kissed her long and hard, tasting of her sweet flavor. "I love you, too. And I'm so glad I woke up one morning between two women to find a bottle on my doorstep."

"Between *two* women?" she screeched.

He chuckled and stood up. Bending, he gathered her into his arms and swept her off her feet. "Yeah, Lacy and Candy. But I tell you what, there wasn't a woman out there that could ever make me forget you. I tried like hell, but you were in my blood, woman."

She snickered. "Woman?"

"Yep," he said, carrying her across the sliding glass door threshold to the bed. "You my woman," he grunted like a savage, eliciting a squeal from her. "Me Tarzan, you Jewel." He dropped her on the bed and pounded on his chest with a roar. Jewel's delighted giggles filled the room—until he unfastened his jean shorts and his half-hard erection sprang free. "And Tarzan going to have fiancée's pussy before cock explodes."

* * * * *

Jennie rapped on the door.

"I don't know why we're knocking when we can just"—Luke snapped his fingers—"pop right in."

"Because, you big lout," she said, whacking him across the arm. "They're no longer in our jurisdiction. Yes, we can still use our magic, but they've given me a very valuable gift. One-half of that one required mission, thanks to them, is now successfully completed. One more, Luke. Just one more successful mission and we're home free. No more worries about me having to be banished back to the bottle for good."

Luke sighed, listening to the footfalls on the opposite side of the suite door as they approached. "Thank the stars."

Jennie beamed, noting Luke's use of that Xanthian phrase of relieved expression.

The door swung open. Vince clutched the doorknob and leaned into the solid wood panel. Jennie noted with smug satisfaction the smudged lipstick marks trailing down over his wide chest and disappearing into his unfastened shorts. His dark hair stood on end, and she knew that style, one that spoke of frantic female hands combing through its thickness during lovemaking. Pride swelled in her chest. She'd completed her first assignment, and she knew without a doubt that promotion of carnality, along with the inevitable conclusion of love, had truly become her purpose in life. She was determined to move beyond that next crucial mission in order to finally relax in the throes of carnal devotion.

But first, before bringing on the next subjects, she and Luke had heard a calling from these two.

"Jennie, Luke. Hello. What brings you two here?" Vince's eyes snapped. "Don't tell me you've come to throw us back out into the wilderness. Um, if so, you can forget it. We're quite enjoying a comfortable bed, food, water," he grinned, "and great sex."

Jennie stepped into the suite, breezing by him. Luke followed. "Of course not. We...gathered, somehow, that you two were just discussing a fantasy. We've come to help you fulfill it."

* * * * *

Jewel watched from her place on the balcony as Vince turned and closed the door hesitantly behind him. "Are you serious?"

"As heart failure," Luke chimed in. "You are, after all, on an island where fantasies are fulfilled and carnality is the main objective." Plopping down on the oversized rust sofa, he propped his feet on the cherry wood coffee table. He was no longer dressed in the toga Jewel had seen him in earlier that day. Now in trousers and a bright green polo shirt sporting the Carnal Island logo, he looked every bit the relaxed businessman just walking off the golf course after a successful win. Jennie's shirt matched Luke's, though she wore tiny white dungaree shorts that accentuated her petite shape and left one wondering if her long, lean, tanned legs were never-ending.

Jewel had heard their exchange, and her heart palpated with a mixture of embarrassment and excitement. Already, her pussy throbbed as she listened to the exchange of words. And her system leaped into overdrive when Luke stared at her across the room. The hot early evening sun baked down on her where she sunbathed on the balcony, but nothing could have scorched her more than the promise in that look. Uncomfortable, she squirmed when Vince and Jennie both turned to watch her as Luke spoke.

"Jewel's fantasy of having a threesome with you and another man," he said to Vince, "is not out of the realm of possibilities."

Lying on her stomach on the lounge chair, Jewel gasped and planted her face in her hands. Was there anything sacred with these two genies? she thought with horror. Unable to resist, she peeped between her splayed fingers.

Vince shook his head. "No, man. A fantasy like that is best kept as a fantasy. I just got her back. I'm not losing her to a stranger. She's all mine."

The bold statement of possessiveness made Jewel's breath catch in her chest. Love swelled in her heart. She lowered her hands and her gaze captured Vince's.

"Even if we can make it so the other man isn't a *real* man?" Jennie asked.

Vince tore his gaze from her and stared at Jennie. "What?"

Jennie rose and strolled across the room until she stood in the open patio doorway. A balmy breeze ruffled her long midnight hair. She looked intently at Jewel, her pale brown eyes gleaming like two gold coins.

"Remember? We're magic. Jewel..." She glided out onto the terrace, plucked up the bottle of coconut tanning oil and dribbled some in her palm. Kneeling beside Jewel, she smeared the oil on her back, kneading as she did so. A flood of goose bumps washed over her skin and up into the hairs at the back of her head. Immediately, she was aware of every muscle, every cell in her body as it came to life.

"I know you think Luke is attractive," Jennie said, leaning down to speak cryptically in Jewel's ear. "I can clone him just for that purpose, just for you and Vince. How does that sound?" she asked, untying the string of her bikini top.

By this time, Luke and Vince had moved out onto the deck. They both stood there watching intently as Jennie slathered oil onto Jewel's back. With an involuntary whimper, she noted the fullness in both of their pants.

Clamping her muscles against the flood of cream between her legs, she replied on a pant, "I only want Vince. It's just a fantasy, nothing more."

"And you're here," Jennie coaxed, sliding down the bikini bottom, "to fulfill a fantasy. First, the goal was to get your man back. Check." She smacked Jewel's ass lightly, and hot darts of fire settled into her pussy. "Mission complete. Now's your chance to fulfill that one that's always plagued you ever since you can remember." Hot sunrays bathed her naked ass. Soft, feminine hands slithered down to cup her butt cheeks and smooth the grease in circular motions over the mounds. The sun warmed her, but nothing could heat up her system like seeing those two hard cocks straining against cloth while practiced hands enticed her backside.

"But...but I don't want to be unfaithful to him."

Vince smiled at her, even as he began to massage his cock through the shorts.

Luke followed suit.

"No, no," Jennie said gently, her hand slipping down to play with Jewel's hole. "I'm going to clone Luke. The copy of him won't be a real human being. You will get to fuck him and be fucked by both him and Vince at the same time, without the worry of infidelity. Think of the cloned Luke as you might one of your toys."

Jewel gasped at both her telling words and the first-ever sensation of a gentle female finger sinking into her.

"That's right, Jewel. The vibrators and dildos you have hidden beneath your mattress at the convent. When you fuck Luke's clone, it will be exactly like fucking yourself with a fake cock. Because he won't be real, just as your toys aren't real people."

Vince stared at her, his eyes glazed with lust. "It's your decision, babe," he panted as he released his cock and stroked it right there before the whole world to see.

God, this was turning her on more than she ever thought it could. Inhibitions suddenly to the wayside, Jewel clarified, "So I can have a threesome without the guilt and worry? No foreign semen, no emotions, just all good, clean, toy-like sex?"

"Exactly." Jennie ripped her finger from Jewel and stood, towering over her. "Say the word and carnal fulfillment is all yours."

She glanced up at Vince. His jaw clenched with rigid restraint as he fondled himself. Luke remained with his clothes on, but he rubbed himself, too, watching as Jennie slowly disrobed. Her caramel skin gleamed in the evening sun.

"Remember, Jewel," Luke warned. "I can read your mind, so no need to put on false airs."

She ignored him and glanced back at Vince. "Vince, you're okay with this?"

He nodded vigorously, and a sort of a strangled moan escaped his clamped lips.

"Out here, where everyone can see?" Jewel scanned the rowdy crowd of people below, all in various stages of undress.

Jennie let out a throaty laugh. "Oh, yes, Jewel. It will further enhance your pleasure. To watch and be watched...it's like two fantasies fulfilled in one. Just you wait and see."

Nerves danced in her belly. Even as she hesitated, she knew what her answer would be. "Okay, but only if it's not real. Promise me."

Jennie crossed her heart. "I swear on Queen Justina's immortal life."

"Well..." Jewel said hesitantly. "I don't know who Queen Justina is, but I get the distinct impression she's pretty important."

Jennie merely nodded, her black slash of eyebrows arching with emphatic certainty.

"All right, I'm taking you at your word."

Vince blew out a breath. "Oh, *yes*," he sighed, closing his eyes with anticipation.

Luke clapped him on the back. "Just like the old college days, huh, buddy?"

He slanted a look at his long-time friend. "No, Luke. Nothing will compare to sharing this with Jewel. I love her, and I want what she wants only."

The declaration only underscored her decision. Certain now, she stood and said to Jennie, "Well, what are you waiting for?"

A twinkle of satisfaction lit Jennie's eyes, and she crossed to where Luke stood. She swiped her hands down and up the length of him, ridding him of his clothes in one magic sweep of the hand. Tilting her head back, she pinched her nipples and began to chant.

"The arrow is straight, true to the heart, duplicate this god, for this we do start."

Vince stepped up behind Jewel, and together, they watched, fascinated, as Jennie continued her ritual. A glimmering cloud of star-like, multi-colored lights appeared around the pair. Luke stood tall and proud and naked, waiting for his wife to complete the spell.

"Oh Xanthian queen, hear me I pray," she sang, her voice rising as the wind stirred around them. "Impart in me powers, love and lust, this day. Woman to man, and man again, copy him, oh supreme one, turn this man to men!"

A jagged jolt of silver light streaked down and struck Luke in the chest. From there, it snaked out and jolted up and down Jennie's body. Luke slumped, and when his body straightened, Jewel narrowed her gaze sure she needed her glasses to bring the apparition into correct focus. Rubbing her eyes, she stared in awe. Jennie had vanished, and in her place, Luke's exact copy stood proud, tall and oh-so handsome. The real Luke stepped forward and draped his arm buddy-like over the fake Luke's shoulders—or rather, over the shoulders of Jennie in disguise as Luke.

Gesturing toward the clone, Luke replied with a wicked grin, "She's...um, I mean, *he's* all yours."

Vince nudged her forward. "Go ahead, it's okay, babe."

Taking three slow steps, she stared, dumbfounded. This couldn't be happening, she thought, lust curling in her gut. It felt much like waking up on Christmas morning to find exactly what she'd fantasized about, lying beneath the tree. Every last gift on her wish list there at her disposal. His chest, wide and virtually hairless, seemed to call to her to touch, to explore. She raised a hand and trailed it down across one taut nipple, down over bronzed pecs and abs, until she reached the erect cock. Suddenly brave and driven by the incessant ache in her womb, she closed her hand over the length of it. The clone hissed in a breath, so real, it made her briefly wonder if she'd been duped. But a quick glance over his shoulder told her that the real Luke still existed. In fact, he leaned lazily against the railing watching Jewel's every move.

Jewel heard Vince groan behind her. She whimpered when he reached around to cup her already tingling breasts. Pressing his now naked body against her backside, she rejoiced, energized that he joined her in the dream.

"How do you want it, Jewel? It's your fantasy." One hand slid down and located her hard bud. She gasped when Vince swirled his finger around it, injecting her with renewed passion. "Do you want to be fucked while you give one of us one of your excellent blowjobs?"

"No," she panted, her eyelids fluttering when he slipped one finger into her. She clutched the clone's cock and stroked the long, thick length of it. He let out a cry of satisfaction that further enflamed her. "I want him up my ass while you're in my pussy."

Vince stiffened. "Really? This from a woman who was thinking of being a nun?"

She chuckled and led the man by his dick to a raised outdoor bed, of sorts. Her pussy throbbed, for she knew it was like a stage for all below to watch. She'd noticed it before, and had briefly wondered what it could be used for, but now she knew without a doubt. And a quick sweeping glance told her the crowd had already taken notice of the activities above them. Eager excitement flushed warm and wet between her legs.

"Yes, and thank God I came to my senses," she replied, gesturing for Vince to lie down on the platform with his feet still on the balcony floor. He obeyed and she drew in a ragged breath when he scooted out of the shadow of the overhang and emerged into the sunlight. His body glistened hard and ready before her, a shrine for her use alone. Leading the Luke look-alike up to the bed with her, she climbed up so that she poised on all fours above Vince.

Turning only her head, she said to the clone, "After I swallow him up inside my pussy, get me ready and gently fuck me up the ass at the same time."

He nodded his understanding, and Jewel's labia flooded with another wave of juice when she saw the look of pure lust in the clone's eyes. He reached out and rubbed his large, hot hands over her ass. Her anus tingled in anticipation at the unknown.

Vince groaned. "Goddamn it, Jewel. You keep up that kind of talk and I'm going to blow before I even get inside you."

Her answer was to slam herself down on him, groaning when her pussy accepted him in hungrily. On her hands with her knees bent and drawn up at Vince's hips, she threw her head back and howled in unison with him. Her mouth came down on his and she tasted pineapple and beer. He shot his tongue upward, sucking the life from her. Holding still, she tightened her muscles around him, sensing the approach of maleness behind her. Two pairs of hands stroked her everywhere so that she couldn't tell where Vince's touch ended and the other began. The cheeks of her ass were spread and she struggled to maintain control when the tip of a finger flickered over her anus. Melting droplets of lust fused deep into her core. Groaning into the wet kiss, she inhaled Vince's scent of spice and man, while another man inhaled her sex-scent.

And at that moment of relaxation, she screamed into his mouth when a long, wet tongue penetrated her asshole. Vince's hands dug painfully into her ass helping the clone to hold her open. He moved slow and gentle into her, preventing the jarring of her ass, she knew, for her sake and the clone's. Vince pushed himself in and out of her in strokes that barely receded yet seemed to go deeper with each rise of his hips. It forced the man's tongue into depths of her ass that had never been touched before. Fire ignited there, swirling around in her belly to wreak havoc on her clit. Just when she began to feel the first rise of the orgasm, the magic tongue disappeared and disappointment assailed her. But not for long. The bed shifted and she caught the scent of Luke's pure male arousal right before she saw his large hands slap the bed beside her own.

"Oh God!" He slid his big cock into her wet ass in one slow, long stroke. Her initial reaction was to clamp down and ward off the invasion, but it happened so smoothly, so gentle and adept, she barely had time to stiffen. The intense sensation of being filled front and back at the same time nearly shot her over the edge. The man stilled his movements, allowing her to become accustomed to the new sensations that bombarded her ass and cunt simultaneously. She could feel his hard chest barely brushing her back, could hear his ragged breathing in her ear so convincingly, as if, clone or no, he was truly turned on. Jewel panted, knowing it would take one more single stroke by each of them together to take her to heights she'd never seen before. Her eyes widened and she looked down into Vince's heavy-lidded, glazed stare. She could sense he struggled to sustain his already weak control.

"Ah, Jewel, I'm a lucky man." He drew her face down to his and kissed her lovingly, despite the almost brutal position she found herself in. "You're so sexy, so full of genuine passion and fire."

"Vince," she spoke against his mouth in a whisper. "Are you ready? Because I am. As soon as you both move one centimeter, I'm a goner."

"Ready?" He chuckled, fighting to hold onto his restraint. "I already came once, as soon as you slammed yourself down on me. Now I'm lying here, and I can feel his cock through you, pressed against mine." His breath came out ragged as he plundered his tongue into her mouth. "Just knowing it's turning you on makes me ready to come again, which bears noting that twice in one round without so much as a few strokes, is a record for me."

Her vision blurred at his heady words. The clone rained tender kisses on her shoulders and neck, sending delicious ripples of cool-hot fire through her veins. Vince filled his palms with her breasts at the exact moment Luke's body double reached around and cupped their aching fullness over Vince's knuckles. Four hands moved over her flesh, her torso, her hips and breasts, stoking the flames in unison. It reached an intensity she'd never experienced before. Her pussy dribbled out juice around Vince's cock, while her ass gloved the other man's penis to the hilt. She could smell the mixed scent of both the man she loved and the man who was there only for her pleasure. Longing for a sample of Luke's flavor before she gave in to the insanity of bliss, she turned her head and reached for his neck. Drawing him down to her, she tasted wine and sweet mixed fruit. Hungry for both men, she pulled him further down so that Vince could kiss her at the same time. Three tongues dueled in a flurry of passion.

"Now," she moaned against their mouths. "Both of you. Move inside me. Fuck me now."

Her breath hitched when both cocks partially withdrew. Jarring the coming orgasm into action again, Jewel held her breath, tearing her mouth from theirs. Eyes clamped shut, she opened herself wide both front and back, relaxing every muscle deep inside her. And she screamed when they plunged into her in harmony. Over and over, the waves took her across the sea, spasming in her ass and pussy at the same time. The turbulent rise moved out in delicious ripples to the very tips of her toes and fingers. She heard them both groan, and felt their hard bodies stiffen below and behind her at the exact moment she reached the highest pinnacle of the wave. On one long, drawn-out moan, the three of them slammed into the shore and splattered into a million tiny drops.

Heart pounding wildly in her chest, Jewel collapsed on Vince's glistening chest and pulled away from the clone so that he withdrew from her ass. That was when she glanced over her shoulder to see Luke behind his own clone, his cock sunk into…his own ass? The Luke look-alike remained standing at the bedside yet hunched over the edge of the bed, his hands planted on either side of Vince's legs.

"Wow," Vince gasped. "Check it out."

She blinked and watched with stunned fascination as the fake Luke gradually turned into a very naked, very passionate Jennie. Obviously on the edge, they pounded violently against one another, Luke's cock buried in her asshole. His hand reached around to find her swollen clit. It took but two swirls around that nub and they were both screaming out their release.

Below, the crowd suddenly cheered their final approval. Jewel marveled at the fact that she'd been so wrapped up in the threesome, she'd forgotten all about being on display.

"Well," Vince said, tongue in cheek as he gathered Jewel close. "Gives a whole new meaning to the phrase 'go fuck yourself', doesn't it, Luke?"

The End

About the author:

Titania Ladley knew it was necessary to hang up her stethoscope forever and write fulltime when her characters started coming to work with her on the graveyard shift. A pretty scary prospect when a nurse is unable to tell the difference between patients, spirits and her over-active imagination. So for the benefit of mankind, Titania clocked out one morning after working a grueling twelve-hour night shift and dragged her persistent characters home with her. She marched in the door, tossed her bag of medical paraphernalia into the spare bedroom and put her trembling, tired hands to the keyboard. You bet she was scared out of her booty! But there was just no other way for Titania to live---nor was there for her patients. ;)

Happily, Titania's never looked back. Residing in Minnesota with her very own hunky hero, one child remaining at home and twins in college, Titania devotes her spare time to family, reading erotic romances, walking, weightlifting, crocheting and baking fattening desserts. And arguing with her stubborn alpha males and kick-ass heroines.

Titania welcomes mail from readers. You can write to her c/o Ellora's Cave Publishing at 1056 Home Avenue, Akron OH 44310-3502.

Why an electronic book?

We live in the Information Age—an exciting time in the history of human civilization in which technology rules supreme and continues to progress in leaps and bounds every minute of every hour of every day. For a multitude of reasons, more and more avid literary fans are opting to purchase e-books instead of paperbacks. The question to those not yet initiated to the world of electronic reading is simply: *why?*

1. *Price.* An electronic title at Ellora's Cave Publishing and Cerridwen Press runs anywhere from 40-75% less than the cover price of the <u>exact same title</u> in paperback format. Why? Cold mathematics. It is less expensive to publish an e-book than it is to publish a paperback, so the savings are passed along to the consumer.

2. *Space.* Running out of room to house your paperback books? That is one worry you will never have with electronic novels. For a low one-time cost, you can purchase a handheld computer designed specifically for e-reading purposes. Many e-readers are larger than the average handheld, giving you plenty of screen room. Better yet, hundreds of titles can be stored within your new library—a single microchip. (Please note that Ellora's Cave and Cerridwen Press does not endorse any specific brands. You can check our website at www.ellorascave.com or

www.cerridwenpress.com for customer recommendations we make available to new consumers.)

3. *Mobility.* Because your new library now consists of only a microchip, your entire cache of books can be taken with you wherever you go.

4. *Personal preferences are accounted for.* Are the words you are currently reading too small? Too large? Too...**ANNOYING**? Paperback books cannot be modified according to personal preferences, but e-books can.

5. *Instant gratification.* Is it the middle of the night and all the bookstores are closed? Are you tired of waiting days—sometimes weeks—for online and offline bookstores to ship the novels you bought? Ellora's Cave Publishing sells instantaneous downloads 24 hours a day, 7 days a week, 365 days a year. Our e-book delivery system is 100% automated, meaning your order is filled as soon as you pay for it.

Those are a few of the top reasons why electronic novels are displacing paperbacks for many an avid reader. As always, Ellora's Cave and Cerridwen Press welcomes your questions and comments. We invite you to email us at service@ellorascave.com, service@cerridwenpress.com or write to us directly at: 1056 Home Ave. Akron OH 44310-3502.

NEED A MORE EXCITING
WAY TO PLAN YOUR DAY?

ELLORA'S
CAVEMEN
2006 CALENDAR

COMING THIS FALL

THE
ELLORA'S CAVE
LIBRARY

Stay up to date with Ellora's Cave Titles
in Print with our Quarterly Catalog.

To RECIEVE A CATALOG,
SEND AN EMAIL WITH YOUR NAME
AND MAILING ADDRESS TO:

CATALOG@ELLORASCAVE.COM
OR SEND A LETTER OR POSTCARD
WITH YOUR MAILING ADDRESS TO:
CATALOG REQUEST
c/o ELLORA'S CAVE PUBLISHING, INC.
1337 COMMERCE DRIVE #13
STOW, OH 44224

Printed in the United States
34142LVS00002B/1-60

9 781419 952258